THE SATAN TRAP

"I slipped through the panel and found myself in a divorce detective's dream world. If it couldn't be videotaped, voice-taped or filmed from the equipment in this room, it didn't exist.

One whole wall was stocked with video cassettes labeled with names, dates, and succinct descriptions of their contents. The names read like an international social register, and the descriptions would shock a pornographer.

If these people were being blackmailed, I had a hunch it was for more than cold cash . ."

THE SATAN TRAP

Nick Carter

Star

A STAR BOOK

published by

the Paperback Division of
W. H. ALLEN & Co. Ltd

A Star Book

Published in 1982
by the Paperback Division of
W. H. Allen & Co. Ltd
A Howard and Wyndham Company
44 Hill Street, London W1X 8LB

Printed and bound in Great Britain by
Cox & Wyman Ltd, Reading

ISBN 0 352 31114 2

THE SATAN TRAP

CHAPTER ONE

The dusty, sun-baked street was quiet. Not unusual for eight o'clock on a Sunday morning. But, if everything happened as we had been told, all hell would break loose in the next hour.

I sipped my coffee and shot a glance at Ty McCord at the table beside me. He was doing his job, thinking—and staring down the half-block that led from the hotel to the plaza.

Bells in the church across the square pealed.

"What time is it?"

"Eight-ten," I replied.

"The house of God is ten minutes slow," McCord sighed, and took another tongue-burning sip of his coffee. We were both on our third cup.

Ty was precise. So was I. In our work you were precise or you were dead. He was CIA assigned to this project as an observer and advisor.

What was I doing here? I wasn't too sure.

"Just observe! See what you can see!" Hawk had said five days earlier at the AXE headquarters on

Washington's Dupont Circle. "There may be nothing to it—for us, I mean—but if there is, you'll need background."

The "us" was AXE, a supersecret organization a step away from CIA and FBI. That step being above or below, depending on how you view an organization whose operatives have Killmaster status.

Without knowing exactly why I *was* along, Ty gave me the details on the plane coming down. Terrorism is practically an everyday world disease now. Usually it's been random, and originating from the Near East.

Lately there seemed to be a pattern, and the pattern pointed toward creating revolution in various key countries. In the past two months, an oil tanker had been blown up, an airplane hijacked with a high-ranking French Canadian official aboard, a series of bank robberies in France that led to a gigantic arms sale to South American rebels, and now the reason for our being in Manaxachuan, a tiny Andean village.

In less than an hour, Perfiro Diaz, the man challenging the reign of the country's current El Presidente, would be standing in that plaza sixty yards from us.

Manaxachuan was just one whistle stop Diaz would make in his six-month campaign for the presidency. He would be in the square less than twenty minutes.

Not long.

But long enough for someone to put a bullet through his brain.

That's the tip McCord's superiors had gotten

and they had passed it along to my boss, David Hawk, since AXE had been following the latest pattern of terrorism and had requested all details.

Ergo, Nick Carter, N3, Killmaster, was currently sitting beside Ty McCord to observe what we hoped would be an abortive assassination attempt on the life of Perfiro Diaz.

Diaz normally wouldn't interest our people; alive, that is. Dead, he just might create a few problems. He leaned heavily left, and his speeches bore several traits of Marxist-Leninist philosophy. If elected, he might very well veer the country toward socialism, if not communism itself.

Then why should our state department worry about keeping him alive?

Because he was the darling—nay, the savior—of the peasant and working classes. Alive he might lead the masses to the very doorstep of the presidential palace.

But the chances of getting inside were very slim.

But dead, particularly assassinated, his martyrdom could become a rallying cry for full-scale revolution.

All this McCord had explained to the powers that be when we arrived. But that's all he could do . . . explain. Neither of us could meddle, only advise. So Diaz's security was up to the current government and his own party. McCord could only hope that they heeded his "advice" and believed the reliability of our information.

I signaled the waiter for refills and tugged the skimpy shirt from my body. It was already hot. In another hour it would be sweltering. I resisted the impulse to lift my trousers and scratch under

Wilhelmina's holster attached to my right leg.

Wilhelmina is my best girl, a very efficient 9mm Luger. Her cohort, Hugo, a pencil-thin deadly stiletto, resided against my left leg. Usually they were under my left armpit and against my right forearm, both hidden under a jacket. But wearing a jacket in this kind of heat would have made me stand out like a polar bear in South Africa.

"What time is it?"

"Eight-thirty," I replied.

"He's late. Maybe they tried for him on the road."

"That wouldn't prove much, if they really wanted to blame it on the current party in power."

McCord nodded, lit a cigarette, and returned to his study of the square. The waiter refilled the cups and left. I leaned back and waited.

Manaxachuan wasn't the type of town or village you'd find listed in any travel folder. It was born old. Viewed from where I sat on the hotel veranda, the town crept out in shacks over hills that were cut up into ravines and rugged, heaving slopes. It had the appearance of a populated area that had once been laid out with some rhyme and reason, but an earthquake had come along and jumbled everything.

There were no streets as such, merely a maze of narrow alleyways barely separating row after row of chaotically built hovels. And, as all roads lead to Rome, all alleys in Manaxachuan lead to the square.

While the dwellings seemed to be entirely made of tin roofs and rough-hewn adobe walls—facing in all directions, as if a stoned tinsmith and mason had tossed them together in one dark night—the buildings around the square gave evidence of planned architecture.

As I looked at the church, with its massive dome and towering spires, the neighboring monastery with its sprawling tiled roofs, and the adjacent wing of the Gothic hotel, I got the feeling that Manaxachuan had withstood the dawn of a million tomorrows without taking a single step forward in time.

The streets were all but deserted and the only sound was the distant barking of a mongrel dog, or the cry of a baby. At the corner of the hotel, I saw an ancient bus parked under the rambling arms of a barauana tree. Both front fenders were missing and through garish red paint a faded Coca-Cola sign could be detected.

It was hard to believe that any spot on earth could remain this desolate and barren. Manaxachuan seemed so untouched by modern man it was inconceivable that it might be the birthplace of yet another revolution in a long line of its country's revolutions.

"I'm going to check with Pepe."

I nodded and watched McCord's big, angular body work its way down the hotel's steps and across the street.

Pepe Del Norte was the local short arm of the law. He waddled two hundred and fifty pounds around on a five-seven frame and constantly bragged about the only crime he'd solved in his five years as a lawman. It was the theft of a cow some four years before.

As local security for Diaz, Pepe left a lot to be

desired. He did carry a gun hanging somewhere under his huge, overhanging paunch, but I doubt if he
could fire it even if he could find it.

I didn't envy McCord having to count on him,
but Pepe *was* the only game in town. Besides, I
wasn't even an advisor . . . only an observer.

The hotel guests began wandering out for their
Sunday breakfast. There were the Hilds, Bernice
and Hubert, from Iowa. They were a retired couple
searching for old Spanish coins. Farther down the
veranda was a stringer for several American newspapers, James Grebinger. He was a tall scarecrow
of a man who hated his job. He'd told me the night
before that his lifelong dream was to photograph
nude models for magazines, but he'd never been
able to leave the models alone long enough to
shoot them so he'd been forced to return to photo-
journalism to make a living. He was in deep conversation with his local counterparts from the left
and right-wing newspapers.

From their gestures and laughter, I was pretty
sure the conversation didn't center on Diaz's forthcoming speech.

The only other guest had checked in late the
night before. He was dressed in garb somewhat between a celled monk and a practicing priest. I had
to give him credit for his faith. He had to be
sweltering.

A flash of red crossed the steps directly below
me, drawing my eye. She smiled and tickled her
fingers at me in a wave. I tickled back and ran my
tongue along my lower lip. I watched until the girl
—slim, beautiful and dark-haired—had crossed the
plaza and entered the church.

Her name was Maria and I sincerely hoped she'd be forgiven her sins, since I'd caused them. It was all part of melding into the atmosphere, you understand, playing tourist, absorbing the culture to pass unnoticed.

I'd gotten very absorbed with Maria the first afternoon, and we melded that night. In bed she was like a little girl, giggly, cuddling, and warm. That is, until she'd wormed her way under me. Then she was a screaming, scratching, tearing woman who didn't know when to stop.

We hadn't stopped for the last three nights.

McCord had his girl, too—Juanita. But I doubted if he was enjoying the same extracurricular activity as myself. Juanita was his local contact.

McCord rounded the corner of the veranda just as the coughing and sputtering of an old motorcar reached my ears.

"Him?"

McCord nodded and slumped back into his chair shaking his head. "The fools . . . the bloody fools!"

About that time the car sputtered into the square and died. I immediately saw the reason for McCord's consternation. Diaz was in the back seat. Beside him sat a sleepy-eyed Guardia Civil private. The driver was an ancient that couldn't lift his bulk from the seat fast enough to fight.

That was all the security they had given Perfiro Diaz.

"It's as if El Presidente wanted him dead."

"He probably does," I mused. "Politicos down here prefer one-man elections."

"You and I both know, election minus Diaz equals revolution."

I nodded and then shrugged. I was still an observer, and, as far as even McCord knew, I was representing State. AXE wasn't in his vocabulary. As far as that goes, only a very few, very select number of government employees knew that AXE even existed.

I might have relaxed back into my chair but I kept my eyes working like metronomes. "Stray bullets have a way of finding you if you don't spot their source prior to firing"—old axiom from the famous sayings of Nick Carter.

People began to drift out from the shacks and approach the car. In no time, the square was filled with color. Heavyset, thick-featured women in loose-fitting peasant blouses and billowing skirts pulled children along by the hand. Thin, fine-featured girls in tight peasant blouses with heavy breasts pulled young men along with their eyes.

Diaz, waving and smiling to the crowd, stepped from the old touring car and mounted the platform that had been erected for his speech. He was a dapper little man with sad, drooping eyes and a moustache that covered the better part of his face. He moved with a shuffling walk, his shoulders stooped as though the entire weight of the masses sat astride them.

It probably did.

Again I scanned the crowd. Nothing and no one out of the ordinary. Diaz's chauffeur remained in the car while the guard slumped against a corner of the platform playing at being a watchful eye. Pepe and his lone deputy, along with the local mayor, were on the platform with Diaz.

When he turned to face the crowd, the cheering started. There wasn't much doubt of it, this was Diaz country. Maybe the man was safe after all. Maybe the tip had come from the liberal faction themselves, just to stir up trouble.

And then I heard it, above the combined voices of the crowd. McCord heard it, too. He looked at me, a quizzical frown wrinkling his forehead, and then raised his eyes to scan the sky.

It sounded like thunder, a distant rumbling that came booming out of the hills in a steady, rolling wave. I paid no attention until the sound grew. It became louder and louder, as if the bowels of the earth were erupting.

Again we looked to the sky, searching for thunderclouds. There were none. The sky, as far as the eye could see, was serenely clear, a lofty azure above the light morning mist. But the roar continued, still like thunder. But it was a thunder of the earth, not the sky, and created by the pounding approach of something unseen from the hills.

Then I saw it, a plume of dust that grew as the noise got louder. It swept up over the nearby hills and around the covey of shacks at the town's edge.

And then they were there, thundering into the square.

Horses, men bristling with weapons, a wild, furious charge of pounding hoofs that funneled out of the alleylike streets to converge on the square.

Dust and confusion were everywhere as the crowd's cheers turned to screams and the riot of color began to move, fleeing before the lashing whips wielded by the horsemen.

Suddenly the windows of the decrepit bus parked by the hotel filled with faces and extended rifles.

More screams.

And the shooting began.

McCord's movement matched mine as I bent to bring Wilhelmina into the action. Observation was one thing, survival was another. Some of those bullets were singing close over our heads and tearing into the wood of the veranda.

"Oh, look!" bubbled the Hild woman, to my left. "A western show, just like Disneyland!"

I paused in my search for Wilhelmina and pushed the woman down to the veranda floor. Over her shoulder I could see the journalist walking quickly toward the hotel door . . . on his knees.

Wilhelmina filled my hand. I brought her up to join the fray, when a black-clad arm moved into my peripheral vision. The hand at the end of the arm held an ugly-looking machine pistol pointed directly at McCord's head.

I was about to shout a warning, when I felt something hard, cold, and steady at the base of my skull just behind my right ear.

"The table, gentlemen. Both weapons on the table or I'll put part of your heads in the street."

I moved my head just enough to see. It was the monk. He'd become a two-gunned arm of the church. I wondered what church.

"Now!"

There was no way. The gun butts were set solidly against both his forearms. One slight move at a three-inch range and we would both be statistics. I exchanged a quick, eyebrow-raised glance at

McCord and gently set my best girl on the table. McCord's issue .38 followed her.

"Excellent," muttered the monk. "Now, let's just sit back and watch the election defeat of Perfiro Diaz!"

We were observers again.

The square was practically cleared now, except for the riders and a few bodies who hadn't run fast enough from the bus window's barking guns.

Pepe and his deputy had acted far faster than I would have given them credit for. The two of them had yanked Diaz from the platform and managed to make it to the adobe jail before the first riders broke through the crowd. They had already started to return the fire from inside the tiny building.

The operation seemed to be directed by one rider, a big man with broad shoulders thrown arrogantly back and long legs that seemed to curl under his horse's belly. His features, even shadowed under the wide brim of the vaquero hat, were clearly discernible—a mashed nose, heavy black brows with a patch over one eye, and a thick, deep scar running from his collar bone, up his neck across the cheek, to disappear over the cheekbone and into the patch.

If I got out of this and could find him again, there wouldn't be a lot of trouble with recognition.

The horsemen whipped into a tightening spiral as a horse-drawn cart bounced into their midst and jogged to a stop. On the cart was a machine gun covered with mud-spattered canvas. The machine gun was unloaded and placed by the platform in the center of the square. As the crew worked to load the weapon, the horsemen fanned out around

the square, blocking all exits and centering their
fire on the adobe hut's two windows.

The answering fire from Pepe and his man ended
abruptly. I rolled my head a little to test our monk.
The muzzle of the machine pistol moved with me
and then stayed steady.

I think he could actually move his eyes to look in
two directions at the same time.

Then the machine gun took over. Its chatter was
deafening as the barrel sketched bullets back and
forth across the wood planking. Splinters flew and
then the top sagged as one old hinge gave way.

It wouldn't be long now and I knew it. So did
McCord. I could practically see the gears grinding
behind his eyes.

Help came from the last source imaginable. Pepe
started firing again from one of the adobe windows. He was trying to get the man wielding the
machine gun, but his angle included us. Three of
his shots, maybe four, splattered into a wooden
supporting post directly in front of us.

It was instinctive. I ducked. McCord ducked.
And so did the monk. My fingers found Hugo's
hard handle and he was in my hand. I shoved at the
railing with my feet and whirled in the chair at the
same time. The monk's arm, with the machine
pistol barking in my ear, passed by the left side of
my head as I fell into him.

Hugo came up, the stiletto's sharp point finding
the pulpy part just under his chin. A half-second
later it was in his brain.

McCord was galvanized into action before the
monk hit the floor. He tossed Wilhelmina to me,
retrieved his .38 and one of the monk's machine

pistols, and sprinted to the corner of the veranda. From a crouch he sprayed the machine gun, dropping all three of its operators on the first burst.

I was about to join him, when a bulky, raggedly dressed figure, carbine in hand, vaulted the railing behind McCord. The rifle barrel came up to my man's neck as I leveled Wilhelmina and squeezed.

He lurched forward to hit the floor with a dull thud, dead the instant my bullet split his spine.

McCord whirled, saw him, and nodded at me. I rolled my head toward the front steps and he started crawling. We were in the open two seconds when chips of stone, splinters of wood, and puffs of dust started popping all around us.

The rifles in the bus had shifted their fire to us.

Retreat brought us to the veranda floor with only the railing between us and them. The retired couple and the newsman had used the time wisely to scurry into the hotel.

"Look!"

I followed McCord's look. He hadn't gotten the machine gun fast enough. The second hinge on the jailhouse door had given way. It now lurched at a crazy angle halfway inside the building.

Several of the men had dismounted and were rushing the opening. McCord tried to get a burst off from the machine pistol but it was hopeless. One hair raised brought a deafening volley from the bus.

The men became a human battering ram against the door. It gave like paper and they streamed inside, shooting with every step.

The first scream sounded like Pepe and a second quickly followed. Then they emerged with a limping Diza. Blood flowed from a wound in his thigh and his left arm hung useless.

Two men dragged him to the center of the square, where he fell. Scarface-with-Eyepatch, still mounted, spurred his horse to within a few feet of the fallen man and raised his rifle.

"Viva Republica!" he shouted, and put his first bullet squarely in the middle of Diaz's forehead.

The rest of the men in the square, both mounted and on foot, began pouring bullets into the body. It bounced and flopped in the dust like a rag doll.

"I think that does it," McCord hissed in my ear.

"I think you're right. Let's get the hell out of here."

We crab-walked backward across the veranda on our bellies until we'd passed through the door into the lobby. Instantly we were on our feet.

Outside I could hear a shout above the melee in the square. "The American, get the American! Find him!"

"I think he means us," McCord said, and nodded toward the rear exit through the dining room.

I agreed and followed his lead, but with a tickling thought in the back of my mind. That shout hadn't been plural—it was "get the American." As we whirled through the dining room and down the narrow hall toward the door, I wondered *which* American.

We burst into the rear patio at the same time. Two of them were there, but not waiting. They hadn't expected us. I got one with two pops from Wilhelmina dead center in the left side of his chest. His finger did a nerve-reflex number on the trigger and he got one wild one as he fell.

McCord dropped the second with a burst from the machine pistol just as it clicked empty. He did a quick once-over around the patio and courtyard while I stooped to the bodies.

"What the hell are you doin'?" he hissed.

"Souvenir hunting," I replied, ripping open their shirts.

They were there, shining black on the white flesh of their chests: medallions, black onyx with gold trim, about an inch and a half wide and three inches long. I didn't have to inspect them close; they'd been well described to me in the short briefing I'd had already. I knew that, hand embossed into the black stone, was the traditional figure of Satan as a beast, ripping his way off a thin, gold crucifix.

I yanked them free and cradled them in my palm as I held them up to McCord.

"Well, well, that just about cuts it, doesn't it?" he said, tight-lipped.

I knew what he meant. The same medallions had been found on dead terrorists in London, Tel Aviv and Amsterdam.

I pocketed them and stood. "Let's get the hell out of here."

"I'm already ahead of you," McCord said, and moved.

We didn't bother opening the wooden gate in the high stone wall; we just went over it and started running. Deep shadows filled the countless arched porticos; and from each I expected to see an ominous, gun-waving bulk suddenly confront us.

McCord had spent his time well. We went

through the maze of alleyways without any hesitation, and soon we were following a rambling stone wall that led into the hills away from the village.

"Where?" I said, conserving air for running rather than wordy conversation.

He did the same. "Juanita's. Shack. About a mile." He pointed, kept running. I followed.

The village rapidly fell behind us. In no time the patchwork hovels thinned out and we lost their cover. Ahead lay a grubby expanse of open, rolling hills conspicuously bare of structures or vegetation.

"Down!"

I followed his lead and put my gut in the dust. The stone wall had lowered in height until we had to crawl on our bellies in order not to be seen.

I began thinking how ripe we were for a sniper bullet if they had any outlying guards posted this far from the village.

McCord had stopped. I didn't realize it until the top of my head hit the soles of his shoes.

"Got to . . . to rest for a minute," I heard him rasp.

"Rest? Are you nuts?" And then, in the dust below me, I saw why: A neatly stitched line of blood about an inch wide leading right up under him.

I edged sideways and then up to his level. Gently, I rolled him over. There was a hole the size of a silver dollar in his belly. I ripped away his shirt and did a quick inspection. Dust had turned to a mudpack around the wound and helped to clot it.

"When?"

"On the porch . . . when we tried to get off. One

of the assholes in the bus, I guess."

"Real hero . . . just an afternoon jog with a hole in your gut." I ripped up both our shirts and made a bandage.

"I didn't think it was too bad . . . is it?"

I didn't lie. What was the use? "It ain't good." Actually, I didn't know how he'd managed to stay alive that long. A less healthy soul would have met Gabriel the second the bullet hit.

He swallowed and spit nothing at the rocks. "Almost there. Get me on up the hill. I'll make it!"

"You shouldn't move, friend. There's no telling how you're torn up inside." I glanced at the wound again. The mudpack wasn't holding. Already a red stain was seeping through my makeshift bandage.

"Got to. They get us out in the open like this, we've had it."

I looked back at the valley behind us and realized how high we had climbed. I could see the whole village and the square with the dark blobs of bodies still where they had fallen. The rebels, if that's what they were, were working from building to building. It would only be a matter of time before they started working outward from the village into the hills to find us.

In front of us, two hills away, I could see a ribbon of smoke and the glint of sunlight off a tin roof.

Juanita's.

"Can you stand?"

"With a little help from my friends."

Grabbing him under the arms, I eased him up to his butt and then to his feet.

"We'll have to chance it upright. You're in no

shape to crawl. How is it?"

"So far, so good," he murmured weakly.

We began climbing, edging our way over the jagged rocks toward the next slope. We made the first one, went down, and started up again.

"Think they've seen us yet?" he coughed. A dribble of blood appeared at the corner of his mouth.

I was hauling a corpse. But I kept hauling.

"If they did we would have heard by now."

I heard McCord try to muffle a groan, but he couldn't keep his fingers from clawing at the hole in his stomach. "Know what?"

"What?"

"You're right, Nick, I feel like shit."

"You made it this far, you'll make it the rest of the way."

I tried to make him move, but his legs caved in. "Can't . . . no legs . . . they're gone."

"Bullshit. It's only a little farther."

He went pale and broke out in a cold sweat. "Oh, Christ . . . I've had it!"

I picked him up, threw his arm around my shoulders and carried him like a sack to the top of the second hill and started down.

He was babbling. "Juanita will get us out. She's a great broad. Worked a gig with her in Valparaiso about two years ago."

"Shut up."

The shack got bigger as I got farther down the hill. It was crammed into an outcropping of huge rocks, with only two sides showing and open. I liked that. The place could be a little fortress if it came all the way down to the last stand.

My feet raised clouds of dust as I slipped and slid

down the hill. My back was breaking under his weight, and my eyes burned as they squinted into the sun for any sign that we'd been seen. But there was nothing but the rising howl of the wind as it swept through the rocks.

She hit the door when I hit the yard.

"How bad?"

"Gutshot. He's lost a lot of blood."

"Get him inside!"

Juanita was a darkly beautiful, powerfully built girl whose immense breasts were barely concealed in a low-cut blouse. They swayed as she helped me heft McCord onto a straw-mattressed homemade bunk.

Without a word she bent to his side and went to work on him with the calm, cool efficiency of someone who'd seen and done it all before.

I left them and checked out the immediate area. It was defensible, but only as long as the ammo held out. That might be a day or a few hours, most likely the latter.

She was scrubbing the blood from her hands and arms when I returned. McCord was sleeping, his chest barely rising and falling. There was a fresh, expertly applied bandage around his middle.

"How is he?"

"Not good," Juanita replied, matter-of-factly. I admired her nerves; they were as solid as her body. "He has lost a lot of blood and the bullet is still floating around in there."

"Will he make it?"

"Perhaps. If we had time."

"We don't have time. They'll work the perimeter of the village shack by shack."

As if on cue, we heard the scrape of horses moving over the rocks.

"Hurry!" Juanita moved like a big cat. A nearly threadbare rug was yanked aside to reveal a trapdoor. "Get him down here!"

We struggled McCord down into the six-by-six earth-floored hole. I made him as comfortable as possible in the cool, damp air with a blanket, then returned to the room.

"What the hell? . . ." I gasped.

"I'm going out to the stream and take a bath."

She was standing in the center of the room, brazenly naked, hands on her almost too wide hips, with the look of a hungry temptress glowing on her face. She was tall, taller than I had imagined in the billowing skirt, and built like a magnificent Amazon.

I understood her intent. "Do you think it will work?"

"Of course it will work," she sneered, and moved toward the door. "They are men, aren't they?"

Watching her movement, I became absorbed in her catlike voluptuousness, the dark-tipped peaks of her heavy, swaying breasts standing arrogantly out from the slope of her chest.

"Don't come outside," she said from the door. "No matter what!" Her eyes simmered under arched brows while a darting tongue wet thick lips and suggested their full sensuality. She moved ever so slightly, bringing apart the long length of her strong legs to emphasize the fullness of her hips and muscular thighs. "Promise?"

I nodded and she was gone. I could hear the pad

of her running feet as she moved around the shack toward the stream. I slipped down into the hole with McCord, closed the trap and used Hugo to slide the rug along the floor to hide the door.

Then I sat beside the door with Wilhelmina on my knees, to wait. It probably would work like she said. They were men and she was woman.

I wondered how far she would have to go.

CHAPTER TWO

Carnella's Alpine Ski Lodge is designed to cater to those people who are somewhere in the gray zone between very rich and ultrarich. Normally, AXE disbursement wouldn't allow me such shoulder-rubbing partners in such ultrachic environs.

But one goes where duty calls, and this kind of duty, after South America with McCord, was a welcome change.

"Another Pernod, *monsieur*?"

I nodded and mumbled a *"Bitte."* Pernod is far from my favorite drink, but ordering anything else in the present company would draw a few stares. He returned with it. I nodded again and returned to scanning the slopes, the same thing I'd been doing for the past hour.

It was late in the afternoon and the falling sun was tossing color all over the Alps. It bounced off the stark white of the recently fallen powder, mingled in the air and then assaulted the eyes. Even through the banana-tinted ski glasses I could feel its rays.

It wouldn't be long before a light haze would slide across the tops of the Alps and sift down into the valleys. It would totally blot out Gstaad to my left and the spires of Saanen to my right.

It would also make identification of a lone skier on the slopes among the trees nearly impossible. That's when I would walk to the lift and make the last run of the day.

Behind me, a woman's high-pitched laugh brought me nearly out of my chair. Quickly, reflexes took over and I settled back.

To my ear the laugh had been not unlike a scream, the scream of a woman in pain and agony and fear. I'd heard those screams less than a week before, and they had nearly brought me out of the hole in the shack's floor as quickly as that laugh had brought me nearly out of my chair.

Reliving it was easy. In the near reaches of the back of my mind it was still happening, over and over, like a slow-motion film with no off-button on the projector. . . .

I sat, Wilhelmina's butt between my knees, my hands nervously caressing her barrel, while the sound of horses reached my ears from the clearing in front of the shack.

Beside me, McCord was groaning himself awake. Now and then his body would lurch and, when I touched his face, my fingers came away wet with perspiration.

Then they saw her. The shout was gutteral, yet

strong and full of timbre. I'd heard it less than two hours before, down in the square directing rifle fire into the bouncing, already bullet-riddled body of Perfiro Diaz. I could imagine the jagged, collarbone to eyelid scar growing livid as his one eye fell on Juanita's massive, bare breasts.

More hoofbeats, some splashing, as the horses evidently entered the stream. And then voices, low in pitch at first, but rising.

Then the first scream, followed quickly by another, and the slap of a hand on bare flesh.

I came to my feet, standing in a crouch, reaching for the trapdoor. Carbines, machine pistols, machetes, and at least eight riders. Reasoning, Carter, reasoning, I told myself.

Another scream and the muscles in my thighs ached from tension.

And then, out of the gibberish and repeated screams, came clear words in Juanita's ringing voice. The words left no doubt about what was taking place on the rocks by the stream. Her cries were all too clear.

I thought about what she had said: "They are men, aren't they?"

She knew what she was doing.

But then the screams got louder and spaced one behind the other. Little labor pains at the precise second of birth, or, in this case, agonizing rape.

To hell with reasoning. Again I lurched to my feet.

But I didn't make it. McCord's hand gripped my wrist with far more strength than I thought he had left in him.

"No!" he croaked.

"Can you *hear?*"

"I hear. It's the only way. They want us, Nick, one of us or both of us. They want our bodies. They'll need them."

"But they don't need hers?" That screaming was getting to me.

"She's one of us," McCord said. It actually sounded as though his voice were getting stronger. "She knows what she's doing."

She knows what she's doing. My first thought when I was reasoning.

I fell back into a yoga position, half on my legs, half on my butt, and willed the sounds out of the world of our hole in the floor.

"Nick?"

"I'm concentrating."

"Well concentrate on this. Bury me deep, with a lot of rocks over me. They mustn't get my body. They'll use it, Nick. That's all they need in this mess, is an American's body!"

In the darkness, I nodded. His voice faded and, along with it, the screams ended on a long, drawn out, wailing note.

I waited nearly an hour, until after the last hoof beat had died away in the still air. Then, like the rat I was equalling myself to, I crawled out of my hold and made my way down to the stream.

She was a mess, not much of that sultry face or big, beautiful body left to recognize. They'd flattened her on a big rock, spread four ways to four trees by leather whips.

When they'd finished they hadn't even bothered to cut her loose and take their whips, probably too much trouble to clean the blood from them for later use.

Using Hugo, I cut her legs loose first. Then I cut the thongs holding her wrists and didn't look as she slid from the rock.

I gathered all the blankets I could find in the cabin and rolled her up in them. It wasn't easy to find a space of ground between the rocks for a grave, but I did.

I thought of McCord, and estimated the space ... *if?* It wouldn't be big enough.

I returned to the hole and checked on him. He'd bought it. I wasn't sure when, but I hoped it was before he knew Juanita had.

I buried them side by side, close, very close, and began filling the grave with rocks. When I was finished it looked nothing like a grave, just another eight feet of barren, rocky landscape.

It took two days by horse, cart, ancient auto, and lots of shoe leather to make my way to Valparaiso. After a bath and new clothes so I could walk the streets, I made the call to Amalgamated Press and Wire Services.

As soon as the computer recognized my voice track and the clicking began on the other end of the wire, I unscrewed the mouthpiece and slipped in the tiny, magnetic voice scrambler that, like Hugo, Pierre and Wilhelmina, was a constant part of my everyday person.

Ginger Bateman, Hawk's right hand at Dupont Circle, recognized my voice immediately. Had I been there in person, there would have been some good by-play and repartee about the quality of life in her bedroom—a place I'd never been but longed for. As it was, from the field, dear Ginger was all business.

"We're on. You?" she asked, meaning the scrambler.

"Affirmative," I replied, going by the rules. "It's a mess. Hawk?"

"Out of the country. You're on tape. Go ahead."

"All of it?" I asked.

"Every detail!"

Odd, I thought. Rarely does David Hawk leave the AXE offices, much less leave the country anymore. Field work was usually left up to myself and a very few others like myself. Must be something very big.

"Is that all?" she said crisply.

"That's it," I replied. And it was, except for those two or three hours a night in my bed at the hotel. Unless it was directly connected, AXE and Hawk cared nothing about my love life. Ginger Bateman didn't even want to hear about it.

"Half a minute." Thirty seconds, to the second, later she was back. "Carnella's. It's a ski lodge halfway between Gstaad and Saanen. That's in Switzerland."

"I know," I hissed.

"I figured you would. Be there by Thursday next. You can pick up your special passport, money, and other papers in Santiago at the embassy. Ostensibly, you'll be delivering a diplomatic pouch to Geneva. From there you have a week's holiday skiing."

"What's in the pouch?"

"Wine for our man in Geneva. He's partial to a special brand. We figured you might as well carry something."

AXE would do anything to get me into a country. At least this time I was traveling by air rather than banana boat. We both also knew, but didn't need to mention, that the pouch would carry my dearest friends. Airline officials quite often frown on Wilhelmina.

"You'll be contacted there by a KGB agent, code name Clocker. . . ."

"Vassily Dobronovitch."

"You know him?"

"Only too well," I said, smiling into the phone. The last time we had met, it had been over the sights of two high-powered rifles outside an old farmhouse in East Germany. And each of us had been trying our best to kill the other. "Our last meeting wasn't exactly cordial, but I know him."

"Good," Ginger sighed, "that should make contact and identification much easier."

"Do I kill him or talk to him?"

There was a little moaning sound from the other end of the wire. Ginger knew full well what I was and what I did, but when it came right down to hitting her in the face with it, she always got a little queasy.

Maybe that's why we'd never made it to bed.

"Talk."

"Why me?"

"He asked for you . . . specifically. Evidently this mess has gotten to be more than their side wants to handle alone."

"I gather the mess has something to do with the mess I just got out of?"

"Lots. Have you read the local papers down there yet?"

"No."

"Read 'em. Tally-ho on the slopes!"

The line went dead.

I gathered the papers on the way to the airport and read them during the short hop to Santiago.

It didn't take a fancy government reader, a cryptologist, or a political analyst to figure out what they were saying, or inferring.

The right-wing government paper was blaming American interference, in the form of two agents on the scene, for Perfiro Diaz's killing. The agents were presumed dead, and the contention of their guilt would be proven as soon as the bodies were found.

Not likely. One, me, was still breathing and long gone. The other was part of a landscape that hadn't looked tampered with for a few hundred years.

The left-wing paper blamed the current government and party in power for the Diaz assassination. They, too, claimed intervention on the part of American imperialists in the form of two agents who had been present. Officials of the Diaz party were also looking for the bodies of the two Americans.

On page two of both papers, there was a story concerning a shipment of arms confiscated off the coast by government police. The arms were obviously destined for rebel camps around the country. It was also assumed that the confiscated shipment was only one of many. The other shipments had evidently gotten through.

It didn't take much common sense to figure that someone, either inside the country or outside the country, inside the government or outside the government, wanted to get a revolution started. And from the various rebel raids and military retaliations since Diaz's assassination, the object had been fulfilled; the revolution was on.

McCord had been right. Both sides would have liked to have had either or both of us, dead or alive, as scapegoats: flesh and blood proof, alive or dead, that we were part of Diaz's demise.

"Your drink is unsatisfactory, *monsieur*?"

"What?" But I didn't even look at the waiter. A man with a flowing red scarf and a black suit trimmed in gold was climbing into one of the chairs on the lift just below me.

"Your drink, sir. Is there something wrong with it?"

"Oh . . . oh, yes, as a matter of fact. It's terrible. Much too rich for my blood. You drink it!"

I dropped some bills on the table, smiled at his woebegone look, and headed for my skis on the rack.

Dobronovitch was twenty-some chairs—about fifteen minutes—in front of me by the time I got on the lift. But that would be no problem. The instructions he'd sealed into my morning breakfast menu had not only told me how to spot him and at what time, they had also detailed the run he would take down and an approximation of where I would find him.

Besides, that outfit and scarf wouldn't be hard to follow against the snow, even in trees.

My chair was topping the last slope and beginning the down run to the kickoff when I spotted him again. He was digging in hard. In seconds I could see the long scarf standing out from his shoulders like a pennant and sense the singing of his skis on the packed powder at the top of the run.

By the time I had buckled on and replaced my glasses with goggles, he was a flashing blur sailing down the mountain. Vassily Dobronovitch had a lot of years on me and had probably been through as many, or more, body batterings than myself, but he was obviously still one hell of an athlete.

I poled off, leaning and lifting my weight to soften the shock on my knees from the hard-packed moguls. Dobronovitch was completely out of sight now, but I spotted his trail leaving the main run and veered off just beyond it.

Just as he'd mapped it, there was a grove of trees, a wide clearing just beyond, and then another group of trees. I couldn't spot the shelf of rocks beyond the second group of trees but I did make out the twin tracks leading in that direction.

The extra exertion of zigzagging through the trees brought sharp gulps of Alpine air into my smoke-and-city-air-filled lungs. It almost made me wish that I was, in fact, on holiday instead of assignment.

Clearing the first group of pines, I sensed movement on the slope to my far right. It was a ski patrol rescue team, two skiers. I hadn't noticed them before because of the pure white of their uniforms.

One of them waved and I saw the Swiss flag insignia of his armband. I returned the wave to let them know I was in no trouble. I hoped they hadn't spotted Dobronovitch and assumed he was lost. It would be a natural assumption; we were far from the regular run by now.

But then, so were they, which was unusual.

They slid behind a rise and I entered the second grove of trees. Just at the far edge I took a hard right and dipped into a sheltered hollow behind the shelf of rocks.

He was waiting for me, skis already off, sitting on a log. His left hand helped his teeth hold a smoldering pipe. His right held Wilhelmina's twin sister pointed directly at my belly.

"So we meet again, Carter."

"Is that necessary?" I nodded at the Luger.

"One never knows with the two of us." The craggy, square face broke into what would appear to anyone else as a sneer. I knew that on Dobronovitch it was his only smile.

"I'm armed," I said, letting the ski pole slip from my right to left hand and dropping the arm to my side.

The sneer grew wider and he sighed. "Aren't we always?"

I flexed the muscle in my right forearm. Hugo slipped from his chamois sheath and, in the same second that the blade hit my palm, I forehanded the lethal little stiletto Dobronovitch's way.

The blade caught the loose part of his unzippered sleeve just below the elbow, pinning his right arm to the log.

"Very good. You're still as fast as ever." He hadn't batted an eye. Calmly, he pulled Hugo loose and flipped him back to me, hilt first. "As for me . . . well, I'm afraid my reflexes are going. That's why they give me only the routine chores anymore."

I doubted that, but didn't quibble. Replacing Hugo, I unhinged one ski and squatted to listen.

Dobronovitch nodded. A lot can be said between two old pros with a little action and a look or two.

"First of all, I'm against sharing responsibility or cohabiting on any project. You know that."

I nodded in agreement. "It comes from our early training."

"That's why we—you and I—have managed to live so long. But times change. My superiors feel your people should be brought in on this. I should imagine it's because if it all goes boom, and you're in on it, we won't have to take all the blame."

"I should imagine."

Smoke started billowing from the side of his mouth and the bowl of the pipe. I knew we were about to get to the meat of it.

"It was routine at first, a normal checkout on a charlatan who calls himself Count Drago. He is a self-styled evangelist who founded a retreat in France, above Monaco, about a year ago. Calls the place Pastoria."

"I've heard of it."

"How much do you know about it?"

"Very little. Left over from the sixties' peace movement, I think. Back to nature, till the land. . . ."

"Supposed to be. It's what you Americans would call a very profitable religious rip-off. Drago's real name is Rudy Sturgis. Your FBI probably has a complete file on him, so I won't go into it here. Suffice to say he's a product of capitalism, a bunco artist from the old school."

"Why should that interest our level?"

"It didn't, at first," he continued. "We discov-

ered that Drago's "temple" held a regular, weekly,
sex circus. He used girls recruited from Pastoria.
You know how it is, a little dope, a lot of misplaced
faith, and you have true believers who will do practically anything. Drago's disciples do."

"Blackmail?"

"Exactly. A few government VIPs, yours and,
sad to say, ours, plus others also . . . highly placed
officers in several worldwide corporations." Here
he chuckled and packed his pipe a little. "Normally
we would be overjoyed at this show of western de-
cadence. But it started going a little further than
that."

"How so?"

"A few months ago, Drago's religious teachings
changed. He started adopting a hard political line,
advocating the overthrow of business and government through terrorist means. Called it a warning
of God through his prophet, Drago!"

"Worldwide revolution?"

"Maybe," Dobronovitch said, his already-lined
forehead furrowing deeper in thought. "Maybe it
was just coincidence that a new rash of very organized kidnappings, bombings, and assassina-
tions took place about the time Count Drago got
publicity for his preaching."

"I don't get it. You mean this Drago actually
thinks he can use terrorists to overthrow countries,
and then take them over himself?"

"Pretty silly, isn't it. That's what I thought, too.
So I infiltrated. I got in as a failed monk from another order."

"And? . . ."

"And everything Drago and his assistant, one

Brother Pierre LaFarge, promote seems to turn
into revolution. But once the revolution is under
way, they move on. I was getting close to why,
when they made me."

"So you bring me in?"

"You are the only one on the other side I could
recommend," he chuckled. "Just in case the only
solution is ... elimination. Also, just about the
time my cover was discovered, Count Drago contacted a gypsy occultist named Serena. It seems he
needs a few devils exorcised, and she came highly
recommended."

"By you?"

"Through a few intermediary sources."

"Is she one of yours?"

"She has worked with us in the past, but she usually goes to the highest bidder. She can be a little
untrustworthy. That is why my superiors, and
yours, decided to send someone in with her."

"Should she know me?"

"Up to you. She operates phony séances out of
here." He groped inside his tunic and produced a
slip of paper.

I leaned forward to reach for it and felt a tug at
my left hand. I looked. I'd been holding the ski
poles together. They were now shattered, split
completely in half.

Then the sound came, the crack-crack-crack of a
rifle magnified to a cannon's roar by the Alps
around us. It grew in intensity as it bounced from
ridge to hollow and back again.

It was nearly impossible to do any acrobatic rolling with one ski still on, but I managed. Puffs of
snow showered my face as I vaulted under the shelf

of rock and made myself a part of it.

I made them first, one on the slope behind Dobronovitch, one in the woods behind me. The white uniforms had blended so well with the snow that neither one of us had spotted any movement.

I knew then why the two-man rescue team had strayed so far from the main run.

Dobronovitch had pitched straight forward from the log. If the pool of red spreading under his shoulders didn't tell me, looking beyond the sightless eyes did.

Dobronovitch wouldn't have any more "routine" assignments. The back of his head was gone.

I threw out an experimental leg. My ski, two inches from the toe, shattered. The shot came from the far slope. The second one, in the trees, had already slung his rifle and was digging in. In seconds, he would be gone.

And there wasn't a damn thing I could do about it.

And then I heard it, that slight whooshing sound of well-waxed skis over soft powder. The one on the slope was coming for me. He'd abandoned his poles. But he didn't need them. He was good, executing perfect stem christies to give me a lousy shot at his smoothly crisscrossing body. The rifle was at his shoulder, steady, unwavering as his pattern brought him closer and closer to where I crouched, flat and open like a sitting duck against the rock.

He would pass me at about twenty yards. From that distance, the way he skied and sighted, I knew he wouldn't miss.

There was a small ridge, head high, directly in

his path. I guessed that he would start firing the minute he topped it, just before his skis left the ground.

But to keep his balance, on the rise, he would have to crouch, bend his knees, to start the jump. For five seconds I would be out of his sights.

I unbuckled the useless ski from my left foot and went into a crouch of my own.

Down he came, gaining speed and momentum. And then he was gone. I rolled and then leapt, landing squarely on top of Dobronovitch's lifeless body. My legs went around his, my arms encircled his chest, and I rolled again. When his stubby bulk was square atop me, I dropped my arms tight to my sides and played mummy under the shield of his corpse.

The skier was big, and he looked even bigger from twenty yards above me. He was also as good as I had guessed, maybe better. He got off three shots, two at the very peak of his lift, and a third in midair.

I felt Dobronovitch's body jolt three times in unison with the slight puffs from the rifle barrel. I also felt a burning sting along my right side, near the bottom of my ribcage, and knew that one of the slugs had passed clear through Dobronovitch.

The sniper cursed and twisted in the air to get off another shot before he hit. It went wild, screaming off the face of the rock above me.

I slid the body from me with one hand and filled the other with Wilhelmina.

He hit hard but not straight. Because of the twisting motion he'd used to get off the fourth shot, his angle to the ground was all wrong. His

right ski caught and broke away, but not before it
flipped him.

He hit shoulder first and again proved how good
he was. A tumble brought him upright on his left
ski. He didn't even pause, just tucked his right foot
behind his left, dug in using the rifle for a pole, and
moved.

I squeezed Wilhelmina twice. Snow and bark
flew from a tree beside his head, but the second slug
found its mark, high on his left shoulder. I heard
curses in a language I couldn't catch, but it didn't
stop him.

Seconds later there were too many trees between
us to get off even a partially clear shot.

Run or follow?

He was wounded. I didn't know how bad, but
maybe bad enough to allow me to overtake him
and get in some talk before he could try to use the
rifle again and make me kill him.

I snatched the slip of paper, that had already
saved my life, from the ground and buckled on
Dobronovitch's skis. His poles were still whole. I
grabbed them and started side-jumping toward the
trees and the incline. I had poles, he didn't; it
couldn't be much of a match.

I was wrong. He already had a hundred yards on
me when I cleared the trees. And his partner was
another hundred yards beyond him. Both of them
were heading for no-man's land, that dangerous
area of an Alp where avalanches are started by a
whisper and thousand foot falls are hidden just
beyond the next jump.

The foggy mist made matters worse. It was thick
now, and losing altitude rapidly. At the speed these

two crazies were going, even though we were dropping all the time, I knew if they didn't read the drifts one or both of them would buy it.

Me? I had an option. If one of them went over and a nice, fat scream followed, I'd still have time to swerve or stop.

I was gaining steadily on my man, and his partner seemed to sense the trouble. He, too, was cutting back so that the distance between the three of us remained pretty much the same.

I squeezed Wilhelmina again and puffed snow about five yards in front of him. If he thought I could do better he didn't seem to care. He just dug in harder with the rifle and bent for more speed.

But the slug in his left shoulder was telling. I was down to forty yards and closing fast. He glanced over his shoulder. Calm face. No fear, just intensity.

We were in a deep rut now, with Alps climbing into mist on both sides. The drop was leveling off quickly and then we were flat. It would only be a matter of seconds. Without poles and no down slope to aid him, his speed dropped to a third of mine.

Five, four, three, two yards. I released the poles to flop on the leather straps at my wrists and bent low. When I was even with him he brought the rifle up and I unbuckled.

Before he could fire, I did a fair imitation of Maury Wills coming into second base right across his path.

It had the desired effect. His ski slid right under my body and the crack of his leg breaking when it hit my hip was crystal clear in the still air.

The ski broke away and he went ass up about ten feet high. I was up and running by the time he hit. I figured that even with the buffer of soft snow, the combination of a wounded left wing, a broken left leg, and one hell of a fall would take the fight out of him.

I was wrong.

He came up swinging on his one good leg with his good right arm. I was headed straight for him and couldn't avoid it. He caught me square above the heart and jolted me clear to the toes.

I grabbed for his forearm and elbow, but got air. How he recovered I'll never know but his second punch came low, catching me right in the gut. I played touch my toes with my nose and whooshed out every ounce of air I had left.

Impossible. The bone was sticking out of his ski pants below the left knee and the bastard was actually moving toward me . . . on his knees.

Still gasping for air, I waited until he was just above me and reared. The back of my head caught him flush in the face. His nose added more blood to the already spotted snow and he reeled back emitting low, gutteral shouts through broken teeth.

He lit flat on his back, finally out of it.

By then I had my air back and was on him. I unzipped his tunic, flipped back the hood and crossed my thumbs over his windpipe. Leaving him just enough air to breathe and do some talking, I hoisted him to his feet.

I tried English, Spanish, German, and French. I was quickly running out of languages to use, when he started talking of his own volition. He babbled wildly, staccato words pouring from his battered lips. He was obviously telling me anything I wanted to know to stop the pressure on his throat.

I couldn't understand a word he was saying.

But he kept saying it, right up until the time his body jerked like a puppet in my arms and his eyes lost what life was left in them. Again, split seconds after deadly impact, the sound reverberated around my ears.

I moved him slightly to the side and saw his partner disappearing into the mist a hundred yards away.

It was a hell of a shot and, for the second time that day, I'd been shielded from death by another man's body. I was pretty sure the shooter hadn't cared which one of us he hit. Nice, deadly group. And, if they had been able to follow Dobronovitch, they must have good intelligence.

I went over his body; nothing but some extra shells and some Swiss francs in an otherwise empty wallet. Not even a passport.

I wasn't surprised when I ripped open the shirt under his ski tunic and again saw Satan crawling off his crucifix toward me. I ripped this one off and added it to my collection.

Two minutes later I was back on the skis and starting to move away, when something hit me—a little tug at the back of my mind made me sidestep back to the body.

I stared down at him, going over every inch of his sprawled form. Nothing. I tugged him over, onto his belly, with my poles.

And then I saw it, or rather, didn't see it . . . the matching Swiss red cross stitched across the backpack. The uniform was issue, or a good facsimile; the back pack wasn't.

I undid the flaps. The casing under them came open in my hands. No survival gear, like rations and first aid equipment. No battery powered two-way radio. Just a receiver, and an extremely high frequency microphone attached to a tiny tape recorder.

I flipped out the cassette and bounced it in my hand, remembering the identical back pack on the one who had gotten away.

I had a hunch that the whole conversation between Dobronovitch and myself was on that cassette.

If they hadn't known about Serena before, they did now.

CHAPTER THREE

"Beautiful, isn't it?"

"Very," I replied, watching the smelly, well-chewed cigar shift from one side of Hawk's mouth to the other.

At this moment, David Hawk looked like anything but the founder of AXE or the brains behind a supersecret arm of American global intelligence. In fact, he looked and sounded like anything but the David Hawk—the always right superior—I knew. The corduroy jacket, complete with elbow patches, the open-necked shirt, and Alpine hat with sprouting feather looked more like a college professor on holiday than the head of AXE on a mission.

"I came here often after the war," he continued. "I only stopped coming here when I knew my war would never end."

I mumbled something and looked back out at the panorama. Hawk sounding wistful and slightly nostalgic didn't fit the picture at all. But then, the peaceful, majestic scene sprawled out before us didn't fit the reason for us being there, either.

We were standing on the balcony of the Eiger Hotel in the tiny village of Grindenwald. Before us lay the most beautiful scenery in the Bernese Oberland of Switzerland.

Beyond the tiny, shadow-box houses that made up the village itself, rose the mountains: Eiger, Monch, Wetterhorn and Jungfrau, all white with powdery snow.

I blinked and rubbed my eyes. They felt raw. Twenty-four hours without sleep will do that.

After the fiasco on the mountain I hadn't bothered returning to the lodge, for more than one reason: too many bodies on the landscape already, and I was afraid there might be another one—live —to add to the death list.

I'd struck off across country. Marathon skiing isn't my forte, but the distance to the village of Saanen wasn't greater than the lasting quality in my legs.

A rented car took me from Saanen to Spiez on Lake Thun, and I again played the telephone scrambler game to D.C. From Ginger I ordered a complete rundown on Count Drago a.k.a. Rudy Sturgis, his man Pierre LaFarge, and also whatever dossier could be scraped together on the gypsy woman, Serena.

Ginger gave me an affirmative and also an itinerary to where Hawk was waiting; I would travel by rail from Spiez to Interlaken, then change to the toylike train that wound up, up and farther up to Grindenwald.

I didn't ask why Hawk had chosen such an out-of-the-way place. He usually had good reasons for anything and everything he did. And, as I've said, they're usually the right reasons. Besides security, maybe he just wanted a few hours of peace and tranquility.

And, God knows, Grindenwald with its surrounding protective peaks could give a man, any man—even Hawk—that.

Beside me he sighed, then coughed as if he were reading my thoughts. "If all the world were like this, there wouldn't be much need of us, would there, N3?"

The "N3" told the tale. Twenty minutes of admiring the countryside was quite enough, thank you. It was back to business.

I followed him back into the room through a cloud of rancid smoke from the cigar. Off came the hat as he settled into one chair and motioned me toward one opposite him.

"We've put two of our London men on the Serena woman. I doubt if she's in any danger just yet, but, from the looks of things, this Drago/Sturgis character doesn't miss a bet." The voice was back to the weighty growl I knew so well.

"Off hand, sir, I'd say if Drago wanted her it was for some good reason. From Clocker's comment about exorcising a few demons, I'd say he still wants her."

Hawk puffed on the cigar and scowled. "From that report I'd say he can exorcise his own demons." He gestered toward a thick Manila folder lying on the low table between us.

I picked it up. "Do you mind?"

"Go ahead," he replied. "I'll order us up some breakfast."

I thought about asking for a side order of eight

hours of sleep, but opened the folder instead.

Count Drago had started out as Rudy Sturgis fifty-odd years before. His mother was a part-time prostitute and full-time belly dancer-stripper in a carnival grind show.

He had been in constant trouble. By the time he was sixteen, he already had a yard-long record. Armed robbery topped it and he did three years before being released due to age and evident rehabilitation.

He returned to the carnival as a barker and eventually worked his way up to owning several gyp shows on the midway. This led to various bunco and con schemes which soon landed him back in the slammer . . . this time in a federal pen where he met a fellow con man and phony mystic/ spiritualist named Harvey Ames.

When they were both released, they started a religious cult in Texas. Via radio programs and good public relations, the cult grew. When the operation got big enough, they incorporated it as a nonprofit church and moved it to the promised land of religious cults, California. Somewhere along the way, Harvey Ames got lost.

In California, the church grew and Sturgis started proclaiming himself the new Messiah.

Then something odd began to happen. His true disciples, those in on the game, started leaving him. They claimed he was going crazy. Sturgis had called down the wrath of God so often and had conjured up so many demons—good and evil— that he started believing his own spiel. He started believing that his power was real, that he could call forth Lucifer himself to do battle.

In his mind, Sturgis began to believe that he had secret powers, powers of expulsion and exorcism. But he had also started to have fears; if he could call them forth, could he get rid of them?

To combat his fears, he turned to his younger followers, all underage girls. Parents got wind of this, and when the bomb fell, Sturgis became very sane and took off with the nonprofit corporate funds.

Since he had left the country, the local police and FBI reports ended here.

I lit a fresh, tailor-made cigarette, chomped my teeth down on the gold filter and flipped the page to the French and Interpol report.

Sturgis remained out-of-sight for three years. He surfaced again in Paris with an Argentine passport and somehow gained French citizenship as Count Rudolph Drago, mystic physician.

Somewhere along the line he met Pierre La-Farge. LaFarge had a shady record with the French authorities but had never been convicted of anything. LaFarge called himself a Doctor of the Mind, and ran a health clinic at LaPastet in French territory just north of the principality of Monaco's borders.

Soon after the two men met, the health clinic became the "Temple of Saabia" and, not long after that, the farmland around the temple became "Pastoria," a retreat for the faithful.

Because of Drago's demonic and oratorical powers and LaFarge's gift for publicity, the cult grew rapidly. The men wrote their own "bible." Suckers came flocking to them by the hundreds. They began using television, and the flow of faithful to Pastoria became a flood.

By the time other organized religions and the authorities noticed, Pastoria and Drago had become a rich, powerful influence. Nothing illegal could be sniffed out, and soon the Temple of Saabia Foundation had investments in several worldwide organizations and controlled some small corporations in several countries.

I closed the folder and dropped it back on the table.

"Coffee?"

I looked up. I'd been so engrossed that I hadn't even noticed that the food had arrived. Hawk had already eaten and was now chewing on a fresh cigar.

The table was filled with food in the Swiss tradition, a separate plate for each tasty item. My stomach reacted immediately and I dove into a breakfast of ripe cheeses, homemade jams, rolls, croissants, freshly squeezed juice from blood oranges, all topped off with steaming, real hot chocolate.

Hawk sat patiently watching me stuff my face until I had poured my second cup of chocolate. Then he pointedly cleared his throat. Time for more talk.

"Your thoughts, N3?"

"He's quite a man. But I saw nothing in those reports that would tally with or connect him to what's happened ... the Diaz thing, for example."

"That comes from Dobronovitch," Hawk replied, pulling a thin leather pouch from his inside coat pocket. "This came by red-line from Moscow last night."

From the pouch he extracted a thin sheaf of three pages. They were attached with the state seal and even before he passed them to me, I could see the red border edging each page with the embossed "Super Secret" declaration in black.

My distaste must have shown all over my face. Hawk's voice went flat across the table. "I know what you're thinking, Nick . . . they're still the enemy. But a strange situation like this breeds strange bedfellows, and moves mountains as easily as people."

I knew what he meant. Moving him out of AXE headquarters, halfway around the world, was like moving the Eiger outside our window over to decorate the side of Lake Thun.

I held a real hot potato in my hand. It had "Eyes Only" all over the top of it, and no designation as to where from or where to:

NOTE: DISPATCH SYNOPSIS—VASSILY DOBRONOVITCH
CODE COVER: CLOCKER
ORIGINATED: NICE, FRANCE
SUBJECT: COUNT RUDOLPH DRAGO/RUDY STURGIS (AMERICAN)
RE: TEMPLE OF SAABIA (PASTORIA)
Am in. Known as the monk Parjacos. Biggest source of income to Pastoria other than farming and contributions is sex in the form of staged "circuses" in the temple. These sex circuses are performed by young men and women from Pastoria. Often, during them, members of the audience are urged to take part. The proceedings are filmed and the negative is stored for future blackmail use.

One Gilda Morrow, a second-rate film star of some years past, seems to be Drago's connection to the monied people as contributors and customers to the staged circuses. She contacts them with rumors she has heard of a "very wicked cult, discreet and exciting." This has evidently been a tremendous source of added capitol for Drago and LaFarge to use for personal purposes . . . the hiring of what amounts to a mercenary army. This army lives and trains at Pastoria. The other inhabitants refer to them as "The Untouchables." They are constantly around the temple itself and very visible all through Pastoria. As yet have been unable to correlate the arrival and departure of these "untouchables" with terrorism in general or your list of dates.

In relation to Drago himself, have found in him flashes of genius and true brilliance. He is a spellbinding speaker and is definitely believed to be the true Messiah by the inhabitants of Pastoria. However, at other times Drago seems totally insane, and in mortal fear that Satan himself has sent His messenger to claim Drago's soul. During these lapsed times, have observed him as a desperate man, a trapped animal with madness in his eyes. He claims to hear voices, moans of the damned. These voices, he says, cheer him on to Hell and call for the Master to claim his soul.

Have proof that two people—Elma Potansky, a Yugoslav medium and follower of the teachings of Madame Blavatsky, and Victor Feinholtz, a Swiss follower of Alistair Crowley

—were summoned to the temple by Drago to exorcise the messenger of Satan should he arrive. They did get to Pastoria, but am sure they never left. Their whereabouts are unknown at this time.

Have suggested Serena through other parties.

Of late, Drago has advocated revolution by terrorist means as the only answer to order in the world. He has gone so far as to solicit funds for arms to this end.

Should this interest and possible involvement in international politics go any farther, would suggest further infiltration and/or observation to gather evidence for removal by authorities through legal means.

If situation is unalterable, would suggest agency elimination.

I flipped to the last page and ticked off the list of names of individuals being blackmailed by Drago, and let out a long, low whistle. The list read like an international political and industrial Who's Who.

I handed Hawk back the papers and returned his blank stare. "I figured they had an organized intelligence network," I said. "Now I know how. These men and women are in a position to know exactly what's going on in each of their countries."

Hawk nodded. "Exactly." He crossed the room, put a match to the papers and dropped them into the fireplace. He spoke as he watched them burn. "What do you think of it?"

"It's big. But I have to agree with Clocker. It's not big enough for world domination. And, even if Drago is a genius as Vassily says, I don't think an ex-con man has the ability nor the desire to go so high."

"An ex-house painter tried and almost succeeded in ruling the world." He stomped the ashes and returned to his chair. "But I think I agree with you. It is some kind of giant con, but because of its worldwide ramifications, well worthy of a look from us."

"You want me to go in."

Again he nodded, his already wrinkled forehead curling even more in thought. He mashed out the stubby cigar. I held my breath but, true to form, he lit another within seconds. I lit a cigarette in self-defense and sat back to wait.

"Our opposite half, in Moscow, has already contacted the Serena woman. I understand that the terms of money have been settled. Their disbursement will be up to us." He paused and handed me a slip of paper.

"What's this?"

"The code of her numbered account in Bern. It will be your introduction to her."

"Then you want me to go in with her?" I asked, not liking it one bit. "As her assistant, perhaps?"

"No." The frown smoothed out and I knew he'd made a decision. "I think you'd better go in alone. If she's been made, there is no reason you should take any of her heat. How you get in will be up to you. But I think you should go to London first. Feel her out. Make yourself known to her."

"Give her the facts?"

"Why not?" he said. "The longer she lives, the more chance you have for success."

"And if she doesn't?"

Hawk shrugged. "She's one of their's. It's their loss."

That's the way the game is played. If you can't take the heat—man, woman or child—get off the burner.

I nodded and headed for the door.

"Nick!"

The tone was overly warm and friendly, and the use of "Nick" meant more complications.

I turned.

"The French have wind of all this. Since they've suffered as much or more because of the recent terrorist activities, they've taken it on themselves to get a piece of the action."

"They've sent someone in, too." He nodded. "How will I know him?"

"You won't," Hawk said, matching my scowl. "We don't know. And it's not a him, it's a her."

Swell, I thought, just real swell.

London is one of my favorite cities, but not in the dead of winter. The whores in Soho stay inside, the fog is thicker, and nothing is green as far as the eye can see. The character is still there, but you have to hunt for it.

I checked into the Picadilly. It's a perfect hotel, not first class, but comfortable. It's also highly transient and in the heart of everything. It took three phone calls to get our London contact. They were using a four man, twenty-four hour round-robin watch on the woman, Serena, from a flat across from hers.

I got the address and number and rang off. My watch said three in the afternoon. For several reasons I preferred waiting until dark.

London dialing would discourage any electronic genius. It took me three tries before a sonorous, accent-tinged male voice answered with, "Madame Serena's." Was the accent Indian?

"Yes, I'm a visitor from abroad. I was wondering if Madame Serena would be available for a reading this evening."

"The seeress has a séance this evening . . . there would be no time for a. . . ."

"Cost is no object," I said, breaking in, sure I would be hitting him right where he lived. "It's imperative that I reach the great diviner tonight."

"A private reading, so late, would be very taxing on the Madame."

"Would a hundred pound note give the Madame new energy?"

It would. He gave me the address, which I already knew, and the time of the séance, saying that I should attend in order to heighten my spiritual vibrations for the reading later. The donation at the seance would be an additional twenty-five pounds.

The men of Rom would be proud of Madame Serena.

I spent the better part of the afternoon pub-crawling. There's nothing like the camaraderie of a London pub to give you a respite from current cares and problems. I knew that, from that night on, I was going to have problems, so a little advance respite would never hurt.

I also wanted to see if I'd been tagged in London. If I hit enough pubs and the same face, or faces, showed up, I'd have my answer. London has categories for its pubs. There are rough pubs, posh pubs, arty pubs, pubs for unaccompanied men, pubs for unaccompanied women, and pubs for those with crime in mind. But all pubs have their regulars, and a strange face stands out.

If I saw one, besides my own, I'd know it.

I started dock-side at a place called The Steps, also known as the Custom House Hotel, on Victoria Dock Road. It's a vast, sprawling pub, with a raised bar at the back and an assortment of cut-throats right out of the pages of English history.

I've been in waterfront bars all over the world and the atmosphere is generally the same. It's not unusual to see a few arms and legs broken in the loo, or someone almost kicked to death in a nearby alley. The only difference with The Steps is that it can happen more frequently.

I had a pint, checked the other customers, had a blow-by-blow description of his time at Dunkirk from an oldster beside me at the bar, and moved on to West Indian Dock Road and Charlie Brown's. Really it's the Railway Tavern, but I'd never heard it called anything but Charlie Brown's.

Seamen, tarts old and young, drifters, and wizened old men mingled in a friendly atmosphere. I was spotted as a German, an Irishman, an American, and as a Frenchman by a particularly well-used whore.

And then I spotted him: short, fat, totally bald, with a gray-flecked heavy beard. His dark eyes met mine for an instant, then slid to the whore beside him. She was a tie-dyed redhead whose breasts, on the bar in front of her, dwarfed the mug of beer between them. She'd never see forty again. I watched them haggle price, but down deep I was sure the whore would never come down far enough.

He wasn't interested in a matinee, he was interested in me—and I felt I should know why and who he was. But I couldn't finger him, no matter how hard I flipped the index cards in my memory bank.

I listened and nodded through two pints as another ancient beside me explained what happened in India and why we lost the colonies. Most old pub regulars relive their wars nightly.

By the time we got up to the Irish Rebellion, I was proved wrong—Baldy and Bosoms were on their way out the door.

I finished the pint I'd been working on, bought the historian his next hour's drinking, and headed for the door. A drizzle had started while I'd been inside. People who had them were hoisting umbrellas. Those that didn't were scurrying for cover. From the sky I could see why—a good, old-fashioned London drenching was minutes away.

I spotted her on the corner, straight across. The red hair was matting and starting to droop. She didn't have an umbrella and she wasn't scurrying.

I dodged through two taxis and a pushcart before I was facing her, the moisture already dripping from my own chin.

"Where's your friend?"

She smiled. The teeth were black. "Yer me friend, luvvy. It's only a tenner. Ain't got no room but I know a cabby whose back seat is warm and dry."

"The bald one, with the beard. . . ."

"Oh, him. You must be the one he said."

"Said what?"

"Would ask about him. Said to tell ya the Yorkshire pudding's especially good at the Duke of York's this afternoon. You understand that?"

"I understand." I slipped a fiver into the dampness between her melons and turned to hail a cab.

One was waiting. It was that kind of a neighborhood, if you had a suit on.

"Wouldn't care fer a little tingle fer an appetizer? . . . I could just ride along."

The driver gave her a stare of disgust and flipped the clock. "Sorry, luv, I'm all tingled out." I rolled up the window and turned to the driver. "Duke of York's, on Rathbone Street."

The cab lurched forward and twenty minutes later I was standing at the Duke of York's bar, drinking a pint and staring at a portrait of the late and lamented guv'nor Alf Klien. He was framed by a lavatory seat.

I finished the pint and ordered another, my eyes scanning the room. I was halfway through the second when nature started screaming at me. I wasn't the only one. It was easy to find the loo, just follow the crowd.

I waited my turn for a urinal. When I finished, the place was empty. While I washed my hands, my mind cranked away—short, fat, bald, beard. Still, nothing clicked.

I must have been cranking away pretty hard. He was on the other side of the partition staring at me before I noticed him.

"Carter . . . Nicholas Carter!"

His eyes met mine in the mirror and I finally

sized him. He was well on the way to fifty-five now; he'd been fortyish then, with a solid body. Now it was all flab. There hadn't been a beard then, but there had been a heavy mat of coal black hair on his head.

No wonder I hadn't recognized him. Now, up close, it was a lot easier. It was the eyes. I knew their look. I saw it every time I looked in a mirror.

And the voice I couldn't miss. His name was Eric Komand, and there had been lots of moons over the horizon and several bodies down the river since last I'd heard it.

It had all happened in three short weeks, and those weeks flashed across my mind in seconds. It was back in the days when there was only black and white, very little gray. I'd just joined AXE, and Komand was the "N" designation above me. It was a revolution in a South American banana republic that our side wanted to happen.

We were sent in to make sure it was successful.

The whole thing blew up in our faces, but I'd managed to get the principals out and headed toward an air field in time. I got *them* out, but not myself. It was then, green as I was, that I smelled a leak.

They threw me into a cell, staged a quick trial, and gave me twenty-four hours. That night they dragged me into a room, handcuffed my legs to a chair and my arms to the table in front of me.

The bright light stung my eyes, so bright I had to squint to see the glass of whiskey that had been shoved into my hand and the nearly full bottle on the table behind it.

"Hello, Nick."

"You!" He stepped forward until the light bathed half his face. "You're working both sides."

He chuckled. I'd never realized before how evil that chuckle was until I heard it in those surroundings. "I work all sides, Nick. Have for a long time. I'm a fixer. If A wants something done to B, I get a price. When that's done, I go to B and see if he is willing to pay a little more not to have it done. I'm a fixer . . . I fix things."

"In this case, A was AXE."

"Quite correct. And B, our government friends here in this godforsaken place."

"If it's so godforsaken, why do you bother?"

"Money. You deal in lives. So do I, but only when there's money involved."

"Why hasn't Hawk tapped you?"

"I believe he has," Komand said, refilling my glass. "That's why I'm off for greener pastures . . . as soon as I finish collecting my fee."

I swallowed another gulp of the burning liquid. "Maybe I'd like part of the fee."

"No way. You're too idealistic, Nick. You believe all that crap Hawk says he stands for. You're too trustworthy to them . . . for me." He coughed and moved behind me. "Now, let's get down to business. You're here as a mercenary officer employed by the rebels. It's a cover, true. But it so happens you were on the losing side, and captured by the winning side. Tomorrow is Friday . . . you'll be dead by noon . . . unless. . . ."

The "unless" wasn't too hard to unravel. If the men behind the coup managed to slip through and get to the air field . . . zip, they're gone to start the revolution all over again.

"No deal," I said.

"I want to know where that air field is, Nick. You're dead if I don't find out."

"You're dead if I ever get out of here and come looking for you."

"Perhaps," he smiled down into my face, "but I doubt it. You see, I've had the AXE training as well as you, plus years of experience. That, coupled with my total lack of scruples, should give me a long and healthy life. So, tell me what I must know and you're off the hook . . . not guilty. Safe passage out of the country."

I didn't bother to ask if he had the clout to wrangle such a deal. I knew he did.

What Komand didn't know was Hawk's personal briefing to me. Our side didn't really care who won. We were playing both sides against the middle.

I gave him the information and flew out within the hour. They captured the rebels, but Komand's own employers put him under arrest.

He managed to escape and in the years that followed, his own prophecy proved quite true. He fixed things. He sold arms. He disrupted whole countries, for pay. And he was never caught.

And I'd never run into him again. Until now. . . .

Now he was moving around me to the other wash basin.

"You're looking fit," he said, putting his hands delicately under the tap.

"So are you," I lied.

"Money agrees with me. I'm on your side in this affair, you know."

"I don't know what affair you're talking about."

He chose to ignore that. "We want the Serena woman to reach Drago. If she does, you get what you want and so do we."

"Who's 'we'?" I asked, knowing full well I would get no answer.

"Myself and my current associates. We plan on helping you get her to Pastoria. You'll see her this evening?"

"Perhaps."

"They're waiting for you. They got the Clocker, and now they want you and Serena together."

"What's your interest?"

"Business, my dear Nicholas, business. I want what Drago's got . . . but then, so do a few other people. For the moment we can be allies again. On down the road, that will change, of course. But, for now, it's stupid for all three factions to fight one another. You're A, I'm B, and LaFarge is C. I say, let's join A and B and all gang up on C!"

Suddenly what Clocker had said made a lot more sense. Drago's mind was slipping. LaFarge would be the natural to take over, and maybe LaFarge was the one with the higher ambitions.

I threw it out. "And that leaves Drago in the middle."

"Exactly," he said, white teeth gleaming through the dark beard.

"And on down the line?"

Now he laughed aloud. "According to my plan? . . . B defeats A and operations resume as usual. If the plan goes well, that is. If it doesn't? . . . well, that's the game we've played for years, isn't it, Nick?" The smile disappeared. "I don't want trouble here in London. We'll get you a safe exit. You get her to Heathrow. No cabs. Use public transportation with lots of people around. Get her on a flight to Nice. We'll take it from there."

"I have to convince her to go, first. She's been made. I have to tell her that."

"That's your job," he said, the grin returning. "Why else would I need you? And LeFarge still thinks she's just another exorcist in a long line summoned by Drago."

"How can you be sure of that?"

"Because, after you missed, we didn't."

Komand handed me the cassette from the second skier's backpack.

CHAPTER FOUR

I didn't like it: too many questions and not enough answers. And now, too many partners. Whatever Drago or LaFarge, or both of them, were into suddenly looked a lot bigger than we had originally envisioned.

Outside the door of the loo I saw why our little conference hadn't been disturbed: three big mustache types with bulges in their coats that appeared to hide howitzers.

At the bar I finished my beer and watched Komand and company leave. Ten minutes later I left. I told the cabby to take me to the British Museum, west entrance. It would be a short walk from there to Madame Serena's in Tottenham Court Road, and a lot less conspicuous arriving on foot.

I settled into the vinyl, lit a tailor-made and closed my eyes.

Serena was a pawn. No doubt about it. She was needed to storm the castle. But whose hands were moving her? Clocker's people? LaFarge? Eric Komand and associates? Me?

I hadn't even met the woman.

Concentrate!

A phony religious outfit with a sweet, profitable blackmail operation on the side. Rudy Sturgis as Count Drago heading it up as the next messiah. He would need bodyguards, yes. But why an army?— those were Clocker's words. An army that started revolutions and then moved on.

Did LaFarge want to get rid of Drago? Hardly. Without him as a figurehead the whole operation would probably topple. Ergo, no religion, and no cover for what was really going on at Pastoria.

Could Serena be trusted? Hardly, at this point. She was a freelance. That put her in Komand's ballpark. She'd done odd jobs for Clocker. That made her slightly red.

And now I was approaching her with a mutual employment deal that she would have to be crazy, or very greedy, to take.

"'Ere ya are, Guv. But everythin's closed!"

I climbed out and handed him a fiver through the window. "That's all right; it's the outside of the museum I'm interested in."

"The outside?"

"Sure. I'm doing a study of the effects of pigeon shit on stone."

I left him with his mouth hanging open and headed west on a tiny side street. A few short blocks later I came out on Tottenham Court Road, checked the addresses and turned north.

It was a residential neighborhood with several shops that blended into the houses and flats so you couldn't tell where one began and the other ended. Hard, nasal Cockney floated around my ears and I knew the residents: working men and women, labourers who tried to make every minute in the local pub transcend every hour of their working day.

Two doors from the Madame's, I ducked under an overhang and surveyed the street. Nothing out of the ordinary for the area: a few oldsters out for constitutionals, some dog walkers, lots of students.

I checked the office building directly across, knowing that in one of those windows was a man with a high-powered glass watching me.

I hoped it was our man and the glass he was watching me through wasn't attached to an equally high-powered rifle.

I put nothing past Komand.

Back on the pavement I closed the distance to Serena's. When I was halfway there the door opened and I slowed my pace. An old woman appeared with a huge, dark-suited bulk behind her. The woman was practically pushed out onto the stoop and she obviously didn't like it.

"'Ere now, I've got me an appointment tonight, I 'ave!"

"Sorry, mum, but everything's cancelled for the night," replied the dark suit.

"But I got to talk to me Alf tonight. It's important!"

"Sorry," said the man, and the door closed in the old woman's face.

She backed down the few steps to the walk, mumbling all the way, and headed my way. "Ain't fair, it ain't. They get the posh ones and us that knew 'em first ain't welcome no more. Ain't fair, it ain't. . . ."

She was still mumbling when she passed me. I was only a few steps away so I paused and made cigarette-lighting movements until she was around the corner. If the séance had been cancelled for my private reading, I wasn't going to foul the plan up.

Three quick drags and she was gone. I mounted the steps and was about to knock, when the door opened.

"I called earlier . . . about a private reading. I talked to. . . ."

"Oh, yes, won't you come in. It was I you spoke to." The accent was pure British, educated, a vast step from the Cockney on the street and a far cry from the thick-tongued Indian I'd heard on the telephone.

But, I shrugged in my mind, the gypsy followers of Rom could probably be anything they wanted to be, on the phone or in person.

"Right this way, please." He led me down a paneled hall and into a room heavy with rugs and drapes, like the inside of a shiek's tent. "The empty chair is yours, sir. The Madame will join you directly."

Illumination was by candles and just enough to let me find a chair at the large round table. There were four other participants and an empty chair across from mine. No one paid any attention as I slipped into my chair and squinting checked them out: three men, one woman, all well dressed and in their thirties.

It didn't jell, at least not completely. The woman and one of the men fit. The other two men looked like they'd be more comfortable breaking arms and legs in one of the pubs I'd visited that afternoon.

I squinted a little harder but my concentration and my eardrums were shattered by a loud gong amplified tenfold by speakers somewhere above our heads.

The sound was still reverberating and doing funny things to the base of my spine, when Serena stepped through some curtains at the end of the room and approached the empty chair.

She was anything but what I'd expected. I pegged her somewhere around twenty-three, tops, and more suited to a stage in Soho than a séance. A nothing waist flowered north and south into more curves than an Alpine road. The hips were wide, almost motherly, and the breasts, sans bra, did a wild dance trying to escape the skin-tight black floor-length gown covering them. The reality of their size was open to inspection, since the front of the dress was cut to her navel.

Gypsy mediums can have bodies, too, I suppose, but blonde hair down to her ass and a peaches-and-cream complexion just didn't figure. I wondered how she explained that to the suckers.

Saying nothing, she slipped into the empty chair.

There was a moment of silent concentration, and then Serena raised her arms and extended purple-tinted nails to the man and woman on each side of her. They did the same, until the magic circle got around to me. I joined in, and the hocus-pocus began.

In the next half-hour I saw the ghost of someone's dearly departed Aunt Clara float around above the table, heard spirit raps from the walls and the cabinet behind me, and heard what I guessed was supposed to be a voice from the spirit world speak through Serena's lips.

It was all done competently, but not exactly well. If it was for my benefit, it fell short. If it was for the others, they could seem to care less. I didn't get the impression that any of them had a departed Aunt Clara.

Serena slumped from the fatigue of the spirit using her body, and the séance was over.

The three men and the woman filed out after a perfunctory pat on Serena's shoulder, then Blue Suit came back in.

"If you'll come with me to the private reading room, sir, Madame Serena will join us there shortly."

I followed him to the back of the house and up some stairs. The aura was different, no fancy drapes, and the upstairs hall hadn't seen a cleaning woman for quite a while.

"If you'll just wait in here, sir. . . ."

I passed around his bulk and found myself back in fantasyland. Again the drapes around the walls and ceiling. An added attraction were tiny Christmas tree lights simulating blinking stars. Cute.

The furniture was sparse, a wide divan and a table with two chairs, a few odd tables and chests littered with junk.

"Cozy."

He didn't pick up on anything. I had begun to think he was programmed. "The Madame will be with you directly."

The second the door closed behind him, I went to work. Gently, I tugged at the staples fastening the draperies to the floor. I was halfway around the third wall when I found it, a tiny bug. I followed its connecting wire the rest of the way around the wall until it disappeared down a hole in the floor.

I tugged gently and it came out of the floor a few inches. I kept tugging until the end of it was in my hand.

One decoy bug.

I continued the search and ran across an old-fashioned Victrola. It was all set up with a quarter-inch thick 78 that boasted "Sounds of the Other World" on the label. I flipped it on and a few astral groans along with something that resembled a zither filled the room.

I pressed on with my surreptitious snooping until I found the real thing not-so-cleverly concealed in the phony Tiffany lamp above the table. The little microphone could be used for a lot of things . . . including blackmail. I suspected Serena used it to inform a cohort with word codes what sounds and apparitions were needed to convince the customer.

Requisite props were on the table, a deck of cards and a crystal ball. The ball was wired, probably to produce astral faces in its murky depths, and the cards were a watered-down version of tarot, with the traditional batons, cups, deniers, and swords in place of clubs, hearts, diamonds, and spades.

I already had the number of the Swiss account as a sign of recognition. But something—actually several things—about the operation up to that point bothered me: the old lady had an appointment; my four fellow séance-goers looked like ringers; and Serena herself was a little too shaky a medium, even to the untrained eye.

I'm not an expert, but I could remember a pretty fair reading I'd once had from a gypsy fortune-teller in a traveling carnival. I went through the tarot cards and selected the queen of clubs as a significator for Serena: the queen for young women over twenty-one, clubs for fair skin and blonde hair.

Placing the queen on the table, I went through the deck and selected the ten proper cards for Serena's reading. When I had them all, I placed them over and around the significator card in the closest approximation I could remember to the tarot layout.

I barely finished when she glided into the room, once again reminding me of a woman on a runway instead of a diviner of men's souls.

"I am Madame Serena." The tone was very imperial and the hand was very grand dame as it waved in front of my face to be kissed.

I obliged and she slid into the opposite chair.

"I believe you have a sign for me."

"Yes, right there." I nodded down to the cards, neatly laid out in front of her.

She glanced down and then back up at me. But her eyes never met mine. They darted to each side of my head and never stopped. "I . . . I don't understand."

"It's very clear . . . isn't it? Here's your significator card and, to the left, your past card; a reverse ace deniers . . . evil brought about by lust for money. And here is your card for present conditions, the upside-down joker. It represents bad decisions, a misdirection in progress. And here, partially over the significator, is your obstacle card, jack of spades, positive side up. It looks as though you'll meet a vigilant person . . . or one who enjoys spying on others."

This brought a slight gasp and, for a second, the eyes did manage to focus on mine. Behind the vacant, blue pupils, I saw fear.

I stood and gently tugged the tiny microphone from the shade. Just as gently, I pulled its connecting cord down through the hole in the ceiling and walked it across the room. Opening the door of the Victrola, I placed the bug inside and moved back to the table.

"Shall we continue?" I loomed above her. She was visibly shaken now and not trying to hide it.

"Perhaps . . . uh, perhaps I should call Charles. . . ."

"Charles? Is he the Indian in the blue suit without the Indian accent?"

"No, that's . . . no, I don't know." She was swallowing a lot and her knuckles where she gripped the table were white.

"Let's finish the reading." I reached across the table and flipped the top card face up directly in front of her. "Surely you know what he means? . . . the hanged man?"

She knew, evidently only too well. She came out of the chair like a gazelle and bolted for the door much faster than my reflexes. I managed to get both hands full of the gauzy thing that served as a dress.

Planting my feet, I yanked. It ripped in spurts, parting down her front. I yanked harder and she leaned forward, her feet working like the spinning rear wheels of an accelerated auto. It became a tug of war, and the dress was losing.

One final tug brought the dress and the girl, in
that order, back into my arms. I managed to dis-
card the reems of material in time and fill my hands
with flesh—very solid flesh, barely covered by a
very unmediumlike pair of lacy black panties.

And that was all. She still hadn't bothered with
a bra when she'd changed out of the black number
from the séance.

She fought, but there was too much fear in her to
do much good. I got one arm around her waist and
jammed her hard up against me. Thankfully, my
mind was on more important things when the twin
pillows of her huge breasts flattened across my
chest. They could have been very distracting.

"Who are you?"

"Madame Serena," she gasped.

I got my left hand up to her throat and repeated
the question. This time there was no answer at all.
I curved my index finger and thumb around her
windpipe and went up, under her chin, into the soft
part.

"Who are you?" She just stared, eyes wide,
throat gulping, breasts shaking. I squeezed.

She gagged but started talking. "My name's
Janis. I'm an actress and a dancer. I used to be an
assistant to Serena. I did the spirit stuff, floating
and a strip now and then behind screens."

"Who hired you?"

"A little fat, bald man. He came to the theatre
last night and hired me to do the medium bit for
you and then some guy in France."

"What else?"

"I don't know." I squeezed until her face turned

a little blue. "I don't know! I'm scared of him. He said I could have an accident if I fouled up . . . a deadly accident."

"If I don't like what I hear, you're going to have one anyway." I think my voice worked as good as my fingers.

"He said I was to pass along to him everything you told me and everything you did once we got to this place in France."

"How did you figure to pull it off? You're a lousy medium."

"I can go into trances . . . stop my heart and stuff. I've been able to do it since I was a kid. He said that would be good enough."

Sounded logical. Not quite up to Komand's usual standards but then he hadn't had much time for preparation.

"Where's Serena?"

"I don't know . . . I mean for sure," she quickly added. "But she's in the house somewhere. I heard her voice in the upstairs rooms this afternoon."

"How many of Komand's men in the house?"

"Four . . . the three in the séance, and Charles."

"Give me a rundown on the house."

She spoke fast, breathless, her whole body shaking, reminding me that she was damn near naked. She went through the rooms, three downstairs, three upstairs and an attic, she thought. She ended on a wail and blurted, "Are you going to kill me?"

"Only temporarily," I replied, and squeezed until she went out. I deposited her on the divan and checked my handiwork. She'd be fine in five or six hours when the blue in her face was again replaced with peaches and cream. Other than a sore throat and a couple of bruises, she'd be as good as new.

Outside the door, footsteps were pounding down the hall. They're late, I thought, locking the door and wondering if the Victrola screwing up their sound system was the only reason.

It sounded like two of them; one went on by and the other started pounding. I looked around for a diversion and quickly found it in the draperies. In no time I had one wall ripped down and wrapped in a pigtail. I attached the girl's gauzy dress to the end of it and climbed out on the window ledge. It was made to order, about eight inches wide and running clear across the face of the building and onto the next.

I jammed the window down on one end of the pigtail, lit the other gauzy end, and sailed it out into the darkness. The front of the building was solid brick, so I figured my flare would burn itself out before it started another great London Fire. And, before it burned itself out, I hoped it would bring the AXE locals from across the street.

Ten sideways, scooting steps brought me to the next window. It eased open easily and I fell inside, head first. A shoulder roll and twist brought me up to my knees with Wilhelmina in my hand, the barrel scanning like lethal radar for a target.

The room was empty. I hit the door and did a repeat of my through-the-window, into the hall. My man was still pounding on the other door with the butt of a .357 silenced Magnum.

He saw me about the time I was on the upswing and whirled. My shoulder was against the door of the floor's third room. The slug from the cannon in his hand hit about two feet above me and splintered the door like balsa wood.

I thanked the powers that were that Komand's men weren't as good as Drago's while I brought Wilhelmina up. Before I could get off a shot, there was another roar behind me and the jamb in front of my face exploded.

Two such easy shots resulting in misses were enough for old man Carter. Asking for a third would be an invitation to suicide. I laid my shoulder against what was left of the door and vacated the hall.

The third room was also empty. That meant that the real Serena, or what was left of her, was in the attic room.

Everything was chaos. In the distance I could hear sirens. In the hall, I could hear shouts, running feet, and a couple more *phitts* from the silencer on the .357.

I took a quick look from low in the door frame. They were both moving out, one down the stairs, one up the stairs to the attic. I figured that the one going down had enough to handle with my boys. I went the other way.

Figuring surprise and speed was all I had, I took the steps four at a time and dived through the door. The woman was belted to the brass footboard of a gigantic bed. Ol' Blue Suit, Charles, was about to ram a hypo in her arm.

When he saw me, he dropped the hypo and his hand dived under his coat. He was slow, too slow. But then so was I. The business end of a heavy Magnum against the back of your neck can raise hell with your sense of smell, taste, hearing, and balance.

It can also make your eyes do funny things, like cross, change sockets, give up the ghost and roll into the ball of your head.

I still had movement, not much, but enough to get to my hands and knees and paw the floor in search of Wilhelmina. Whoever it was who had wielded the .357 took care of that with a well-placed size twelve in the small of my back.

From then on I saw hazily and heard, barely, everything from a worm's eye view. Charles's brogans, being substantially different than Serena's black heels, gave me some indication of current events. From the shuffling, I figured Charles was unbelting her. Odd, why? Hypo's probably broken, gonna choke her to death. Probably doesn't know a good windpipe chop will take care of the problem. But then everyone isn't as gifted as you, Nick, old man.

I was really getting fuzzy.

Now .357's shoes came into the picture. They both started working on the black heels. It's all over. Lay down and die, Carter, it'll make the pain go away.

Then a big curve. She got away. She fell on her belly and rolled to her back. And in her hands was dear Wilhelmina, jumping like hell.

I smiled, or at least I think I smiled. My neck was paralyzed. It was hard to tell.

I didn't know if she was hitting anything, but I gave her credit for getting off every round in the clip in jig time.

Then I gave up.

I came back with a cross between an amyl nitrate and a sulphur pot being waved under my nose.

"N3 . . . N3 . . . what's your name?"

"Puddin'-tone. What's yours?"

"Where are you?"

"In Londontown to see the Queen. Quit shaking me, my brains will fall out!"

"I think he's okay. His brains might be a little mixed up but there's not much blood."

Thanks a lot. *Any* blood, as long as it's mine, is a lot.

I opened my eyes, blinked, and found enough focus to push the foul smell from under my nose. It was replaced with a piece of embossed leather bearing the Amalgamated seal.

"Hall, London branch," said the voice from the face behind it.

"Any casualties?"

"One of my men gets early retirement from a smashed left elbow," he replied. "But other than that, nil."

I looked past him and saw Serena sitting like a lump in a chair across the room. "Didn't she even wing one of them?"

"It's hard to tell. They both went out the window."

"From three stories?"

"There's a roof one story down. They roof-hopped and disappeared," he said. "Can you stand?"

"With some help." They helped and I staggered across to her. By this time, my eyes were working pretty well. At least well enough to see that this one was a lot more of what I had expected to find in the first place.

The complexion, that wasn't black and blue, was

a shining olive and the hair was shoulder length, straight, and raven black. Even with her sitting in the chair I could tell she was tall, with wide hips, big bones and small, jutting breasts. The latter was pretty easy to detect since one of them blinked at me from around the mangled top of her dress.

The eyes, when she looked up at me, were dark and full of hatred. She followed my gaze down to her bare breast and shrugged once. The material fell into place and then opened again. She left it that way.

I leaned closer and whispered the series of numbers Hawk had given me. There was a spark of recognition in her eyes and then they went vacant again.

"The deal's off." Her voice was low, husky, with a lot of power.

"How so?" I replied.

"Too many cooks in the kitchen."

"According to Clocker, you've been to that well before."

I thought I detected a lip curl. It was close to a smile but could be mistaken for a sneer.

"Sure, but only on my terms. This party's gotten too rough."

I did some quick adding in my head and took a stab. "You're American."

"So what."

"What are you wanted for in the States?"

That brought a little more life to her, but only for a moment. She was good, as good as I figured she would be if she'd worked for Clocker in the past.

"What?" I tried again.

"Child molestation . . . little boys."

Zero. I turned to Hall. "What are you holding them off with downstairs?"

"Dope bust."

"Good." I nodded at Serena. "Here's your ring leader. You must have something we can plant on her." He nodded and I turned back to her. "It'll never get a conviction, but it's enough for deportation."

"Bastards!" Her eyes never wavered as her foot came up between Hall's legs. He went down in agony. She stood and nearly met my eyes on the same level. "I hope that one has already started his family. Let's go."

I was glad I was standing at her side.

CHAPTER FIVE

London's Heathrow Airport was definitely out. If Komand had already planned the departure from there of myself and his ringer Serena, I didn't want to give him a shot at myself and the real one.

A helicopter dumped us just in time to get the hovercraft across the Channel to Calais. There, a prearranged car awaited us, complete with suitcases. The organization can be very efficient when there's enough at stake.

"Get in!"

"Where are we going?"

Those were the first words I'd heard from her mouth since she'd stepped into the official car outside her flat in London and I'd tossed her a whole dress and jacket.

"Paris. Get in!" I opened the car door.

"I'd like to get a bath, a few hours sleep, and crawl into some clothes that fit." She stood her ground.

"Baths and sleep take too much time . . . for

now. That suitcase on the back seat has fresh clothes . . . your size."

She folded her arms and tried to stare me down. "This time I'd like to dress in private."

I chuckled. She's practically given the driver apoplexy in London when she'd peeled off the torn dress and taken her time crawling into the one she now wore. The change from sheer panties to dress and jacket two sizes too large was probably the only thing that had kept us on the road.

"Well?"

"Madame Serena," I said, pushing my already cigarette-raspy voice down another full octave, "I have been days without sleep, not helped by the addition of proper nourishment and the battering and bruising of my head and body. . . ."

"I don't give a damn."

She was unnerving, to say the least. I leaned close, very close, to her face. "If you don't get your butt in that seat I will stuff you into it much the same as a dear old aunt of mine stuffed dressing into a turkey. . . ."

She moved.

I turned to Hall, collected fresh passports under a Mr. and Mrs. Phoney Name, and whispered my plans for Paris and beyond. His eyebrows went up when he heard, but he nodded.

Fifteen minutes later the lights of the port town were receding behind us and I was barreling the little car south on the Paris highway.

"Must you drive so fast?"

"Yes."

That was it for about thirty kilometers, until she again poked her head up from the lump she'd made of herself in the far corner of the car.

"May I have a cigarette?"

I gave her one and punched the dash lighter. When it popped she lit up and inspected the tailor-made in the leftover glow from the lighter.

"N.C.?"

"A special brand. I have them made up in London."

"Nick Carter," she mused. "A little ostentacious."

"Perhaps," I replied, lighting one myself. "But at least *I've* got *two* names." She went back into the darkness of her lump with only a now-and-then glow from the cigarette telling me she was still alive and puffing.

I tried to remember if I'd identified myself by name along with the numbers of her account. I was sure I hadn't, and made a mental note to check with Hawk to see if our Kremlin counterparts had, when they'd made the deal with her.

By the time we hit lights on the outskirts of Paris, I was letting one eye sleep while the other drove, and then shifting over. Just a little longer, I told myself, and reached down to brutally pinch the fleshy inner thigh for the hundredth time. "Ouch." Both eyes blinked open.

"What are you doing?"

"Abusing myself. It keeps me awake."

"Interesting. Are we stopping in Paris?"

"No."

"The hell we're not," she hissed, coming clear up in the seat now.

"We've got a plane to catch."

"I'm not getting on a plane like this." She

and found mine. I held for a moment, then dropped my concentration back to my drink. But not before I again saw a flicker of recognition in her look.

Was it recognition? Or was it merely a roving eye, bored with her current lover and looking for a new conquest? That was highly possible. From the same informants on Gilda Morrow, I'd learned of Paulina Mendici's penchant for new kicks. That information, plus a scanning of the local newspaper after the screen star's arrival in Monaco, had led me to putting the two women together.

Being where I was, casing them in the Casino lounge, was a natural conclusion. Everyone with money who lives in or visits Monaco, eventually finds his way to the Casino.

I stored Mendici's look away for future reference. If I couldn't get into Drago's temple via Gilda Morrow, the beautiful Italian screen star might be a possible alternate.

It had been two days since I had rented the limo and sent Serena, in style, over the mountain to Pastoria. Two days, and no word as per our agreement on a means of communication.

But I'd almost expected it. We hadn't exactly parted under happy circumstances. She'd been right. The night train from Rome had been heatless, not the Arctic, but a close second.

We had tried to settle in with a hard belt apiece from a brandy flask I'd grabbed in the station before boarding. It, and all the blankets we could muster, hadn't helped. Ringing for more blankets had been like trying to raise an already hibernated bear from his winter's sleep. So we lay chattering.

I'd given her the upper because, according to my high school physics, heat rises. That is, heat rises if there is any heat. Since there wasn't any, we still lay chattering. Even total fatigue and another jolt from the brandy flask failed to put us out.

She'd leaned over the edge of her bunk and scowled down at me. "Carter?"

"Yes."

"I'm cold. I said we'd freeze and we're freezing."

"I concede. We're freezing."

"That settles it." I saw a flash of white, there was a blast of cold air, and her cold but soft rear end spooned into me under the covers.

"I thought you didn't like me."

"I don't. Cold feet make strange bed fellows. Put your arms around me."

I did. One breast amply filled my right hand. She moved my hand down to her belly. I moved it lower. She moved it back up.

"I thought you were tired."

"I was."

"You are. Good night."

She clamped both her hands over my hand on her stomach and held it there. I gave it up, closed my eyes, and began to dream of soft, curving bellies.

"Nick?" It must have been twenty minutes later.

"Hmmmm."

"Nick?" She backed up a little closer and replaced my hand on her breast. It was warm and full and soft. I squeezed and went promptly back to sleep.

The next morning I wasn't sure whether she was more angry about my falling asleep or nervous about the fact that the trip was over and she would soon have to convince Drago that she was indeed a medium who could exorcise his devils.

We dressed, ate, and detrained in silence. I hired a limousine, briefly checked out the driver to make sure he knew how to find the destination, and shuffled Serena into the back seat.

She sat in stony silence as I explained how to contact me if there was any trouble before I got myself into Pastoria. I hoped that would be within three or four days.

"Everything understood?"

She nodded.

"Good luck." I closed the door and leaned in the window. "You look a little pale. What's the matter?"

"I'm scared to death, dammit. Drago's a pro. How can I fool him with spooks without props?"

"You'll find a way," I grinned. "That's what you're getting paid for."

I slapped the side of the car and watched her white face roll away through the rear window.

Damn, I'd thought at the time, she really is scared. A hell of a lot of good she'll do me when push comes to shove.

"Monsieur?"

"What . . . oh, yes?" A tall, mustachioed Eurasian was hovering at my shoulder.

"The tables are now open, sir."

I nodded and he moved down the line, informing each person at the bar, individually, that the time had come to give away their money.

Mendici, Morrow and party were already moving toward the lobby. I dropped a few francs on the bar to cover my drinks and sauntered after them. I strolled past well-guarded cashiers' cages and past the huge, curved arch of the "ordinary people" game room, toward the stairs.

The red and gold carpet on the stairs felt immediately different under the soles of my feet, thicker, posher. Richer. And well it might. At the head of the stairs and to the left, around the horseshoe mezzanine, lay the high-rollers' room. To gain entrance, one needed a tuxedo and a two-thousand franc chip—four hundred and fifty dollars, give or take a few sou.

Of course, one needn't gamble the whole amount once the chip was broken, but the house gambled on human nature . . . and usually won.

The room was huge, with high ornate ceilings and floor-to-ceiling draperies that muted the already muted play around the tables. Light from sparkling chandeliers encased the room and its occupants in an aura of understated opulence.

Up here on this floor there were no slot machines, no rattling chuck-a-luck cages, no croupiers' voices above a polite whisper. All was concentration on the action at hand. And the action consisted of three, different-limit craps tables —all going strong; two roulette tables—equally as busy; one of two baccarat full, the other waiting for a later hour when the real money would arrive; and five blackjack tables—spotty.

The Mendici-Morrow party was scattered over two of the blackjack tables. I bypassed them and moved onto the occupied baccarat table. In time, I would move in. In the meantime, I would establish myself as a high roller. A few rounds of baccarat would do that. The game started among the nobles in the Court of Charles VIII, and because of the stakes it still takes a pretty noble bankroll to play.

I cashed my chip and sat down. For the next half-hour I made small bets against the house and, out of the corner of my eye, watched the action at both blackjack tables. People foreign to the party drifted in and out. When the end seat, directly beside Paulina Mendici, opened up for the second time I pocketed my chips—about five hundred francs poorer from my lack of interest in the game—and moved across the room.

"The limit is five hundred francs, *monsieur*. The minimum bet is fifty," the dealer said, rifling cards from the shoe at his left.

I nodded, correlated that into approximately two hundred and ten dollars, and slid onto the vacant stool. Beside me, Paulina Mendici threw a vague smile in my direction. I nodded a bow and she returned to the cards in front of her.

When the round was over I placed a five-hundred-franc chip above my square and waited for cards. When they arrived I held a stiff hand, thirteen. The dealer turned and showed a nine.

I've never fancied myself a professional gamer, but being an avid student has helped me often, even in my line of work.

Old Rule: hit a stiff hand—any combination of 12, 13, 14, 15 or 16—if the dealer has 7,8,9, picture or ace showing.

I hit the thirteen with a six, making nineteen. The dealer flipped a seven over the nine and hit himself with a six. Bust.

I won.

I pulled one chip and watched chips around the table disappear into the dealer's tray.

I won four of the next six rounds, and watched the others lose. They were all merely passing time, rather than gambling.

"You are a good gambler, monsieur," came the husky voice from beside me, in French.

"Just an astute observer," I replied, in Italian.

Play came around again and I saw an opening to prove my astuteness and ingratiate myself at the same time. The first three players on Giggly Gilda's right all busted. Gilda herself took a third hit and gasped.

"Oh, I just can't . . . I don't know, I just can't do it!"

I glanced over the shelf of Paulina Mendici's breasts and discovered the object of the fat woman's consternation. Seven, five, three: a fifteen count. And the dealer had a queen showing.

I dived in.

"Ms. Morrow. . . ."

Her puffy eyes lit up when they found me. "Oh, you know me?" Her voice came out like a little girl Scarlet O'Hara with a whisky rasp. "Do I know you?"

"Carr, Ms. Morrow. Nicholas Carr. I've seen all your films. Perhaps I could help?"

"Oh, would you? You seem to win all the time, Mr. Carr. Do you have a system?"

The dealer groaned.

"No, Madame. My only system is common sense." I couldn't help it.

She didn't hear me. "I just don't dare ask for another card!"

"Quite the contrary," I replied, using my best continental tones. "The question is not should you dare to take a hit. The real question is, should you dare *stand*? And the obvious answer is definitely no."

"Oh. Why?"

Again the dealer groaned and tapped the shoe with his manicured nails. Paulina Mendici's face, close beside my own, broke into a bemused smile.

"The dealer has a picture card up. By all odds, he has a winner. There is very little chance that he will have to hit at all. And, if he does, he probably won't hit into a bust. Therefore, Ms. Morrow, you have no chance at all with a fifteen. You are practically obligated to draw another card."

Giggly Gilda's expression showed plainly that she didn't understand at all. But she took my advice.

Her hit card was a four. She sighed.

Paulina had a similar hand, and drew a card.

I stayed on seventeen.

The dealer flipped his hole card and stayed on eighteen. Gilda won the fifty-franc minimum. Paulina won the five-hundred-franc maximum. And I lost.

The air filled with Gilda's squeals, so abhorrent to the concentrating gambler, and she turned to me. "Oh, Mr. Carr, from now on *you* can bet all my hands!"

"Thank you, Madame," I said, rising, "but I think I hear a cry from the craps table."

I bet straight "Don't Pass" bets at the crap table for the next twenty minutes, recouped all my losses plus a thousand francs, and moved to the bar.

Through two drinks I studiously avoided glancing around the room. There was no mirror behind this bar, so I didn't see him.

"Pardon, monsieur."

I rolled slowly around on the stool. He was tall and had more muscles than his tuxedo could contain. "Yes?"

"I am with Madame Morrow's party."

"Yes." His eyes were vacant, as if he were stoned And the way he said *Madame Morrow* made me look for a lapel button that said, "Resident Stud."

"Madame Morrow would like you to join her party in the downstairs lounge for a drink."

"No, thank you." I started to roll around back to the bar, when a steel claw wrapped around my left bicep. Gently, but very firmly, I was spun back around to face him.

"I'm sorry, but I usually bring back what the Madame sends me for."

I tensed my bulging muscle under his hand. His hand easily untensed it and just as easily lifted me off the stool and onto the floor.

"I think you heard me," I hissed, two inches from his face. "I said 'no, thank you,' that's what I meant."

He smiled. His teeth were very even, very perfect, and gleamed very white in the darkly tanned face. I thought of displacing a few of them when he pulled me up close and my own hands came against his belly about beltline.

"Shall we go?" he said, still smiling.

I curled my fingers under his tux vest and grabbed two handsful of belt and pants. I yanked upward with all the strength in my upper torso. He came off the floor a good three inches and I knew the seam in his crotch had done an even better job than my knee could have performed.

When he came down, the smile was gone and his face was tanless. The steel claw had also released my arm and now dangled at his side. From the way his hands trembled I knew he wanted to grab his crotch. But pride held him back.

"Can you hear me?" I whispered close to his ear.

Something resembling, "Uggaawww," came from his throat and I yanked again. When he came down this time, pride be damned. He grabbed his crotch and his thighs slapped protectively together. His lips also muttered a rather strangled, "Oui."

"You tell Madame Morrow that I don't accept invitations from lackeys or little boys. You also tell Madame Morrow that if she wants to join me, I'll be in the downstairs lounge, at the bar, and she's buying. Now toddle along!"

He moved away. I noticed that he'd bravely brought his hands back to his sides, but his legs were still very much together and he was taking very short steps.

I retraced my steps down the stairs and into the main floor lounge. I ordered a Scotch at the bar and had half a drink, when I felt her slide onto the stool beside me.

"Buy a girl a drink?" It was in English. "I heard that in an American movie once."

I swiveled my head just as she crossed her shapely legs. I hadn't noticed the slit in the skirt before. Now it was very evident and a finely textured white thigh shown through it.

"You speak English?"

"I have to. I often dub my own films for the American and English market."

"What would you like to drink?"

"A Pernod, but I'd rather drink it in my car. It's right outside."

"Are we going any place in particular?"

"Up the coast . . . to Gilda's," she replied, placing a cigarette in her lips and letting it dangle. "She's showing a film."

I lit it and watched the top of her expand out of her dress as she got it going. "I turned that invitation down a little earlier."

"I know," she smiled. "That's why I'm making it now. Adoreman. . . ."

"Adoreman?"

She chuckled. "The lackey you sent back. He relayed your message quite emphatically." There was another chuckle. "You've probably ruined Gilda's sex life for a month."

"Did she send you?" I asked.

"No. The invitation came from me in the first place." She mashed the cigarette into an ashtray and stood. "Shall we go?"

I guided her by the elbow through the room. "I hope the film is dirty."

"Oh, it is," Paulina replied. "It's one of Gilda's early ones."

CHAPTER SIX

"Ah, how sad when time passes. I weighed a mere one hundred and ten pounds then . . . I was a sylphan little doll! And off-screen I was always dressed in white, with blue trim and blue slippers. They adored me, gave me constant parties. At one gala in Italy they made a life-sized statue of me in shaved ice to cool the champagne! And champagne there was in those days, oceans of it . . . French, icy and bubbly! I drank tons of it and danced all night. . . ."

Gilda Morrow went on and on and on. She'd been going on since the old, cracked film had first started flickering on the screen.

We were about an hour into it now and I hoped it was drawing toward the end. I'd already cased the situation pretty well and decided that Gilda Morrow didn't care for me or trust me. But she had

a big fish on the hook in the form of Paulina Mendici.

When the Italian woman had moved right in
beside me on one of the many couches facing the
screen, I decided she would be a better entree into
Pastoria than Gilda. When she'd taken my arm
and cradled it against one of her ample breasts, I
knew it.

Gilda started again. "Look at that . . . I was a
mere wisp in his arms! It will happen to you some-
day, too, my sweet Paulina!"

My arm was squeezed a little tighter and, under
her breath, I heard Paulina whisper, *"Merde!"*

I concentrated on the screen, for safety's sake if
nothing else. Gilda's rantings were true, to a
degree. She had been petite and beautiful in those
days. The film was the Hundred and Tenth Return
of the Vampire, or something close. I couldn't remember the exact title.

The tall, cloaked figure was carrying Gilda down
a long flight of castle stairs. At the bottom were
two open coffins. The Dracula figure was vaguely
familiar but I couldn't place him.

Then there was a cut to the handsome blond
hero galloping through the woods, with a hammer
in one hand and a stake in the other.

Back to Dracula. This time a close-up as he deposited Gilda in the coffin. I'll say one thing, he
was perfect for the role. With his long, sallow face,
evil dark eyes, the thin, craggy features with a wide,
unsmiling mouth, and mane of thick black hair,
they probably didn't even have to make him up.

Then I saw it. The ring. It practically filled the
screen as he caressed Gilda's neck. It was large,

with a blood red stone. But in the center of the stone was the duplicate of the medallions I'd seen before, the beast of Satan wrenching himself from a golden cross.

I was about to mention it to Gilda, during one of her quiet moments, when the hero burst through the door and all hell broke loose on screen.

"Now the bastard gets it!" Gilda hissed. I glanced at her briefly and saw pure hate—real hate, not movie-make-believe hate—mirrored on her fat little face.

To the accompaniment of booming, strident music, the hero backed Dracula to the wall. After a brief skirmish the stake found its mark and Dracula was dust.

On cue, Gilda awoke and together she and the hero walked from the crypt into the rising sun and the dawn of a new day.

As the music peaked, Gilda and her male entourage applauded, Paulina yawned, and I lit a cigarette and mulled over what ready excuse I could make to get out of there with Paulina.

I needn't have bothered. She did it for me, fast. Actually, too fast. I'd wanted to lightly question Gilda about the actor who'd played the vampire. It proved impossible. Guiding me quickly to the door, Paulina was arguing that since we were both staying at the Hotel de Paris, she would drop me. And Gilda was on her same kick: "One hundred and ten pounds in those days. Oh, I was so popular, Paulina. Almost as much as you are now. I must have lost my virginity at least a hundred times!"

"That reminds me," Paulina replied and the two

of them went into a quick, hushed conference. There seemed to be an agreement of sorts, with a lot of giggling and waving of fat, diamonded fingers on Gilda's part.

Then I was being guided down the drive and back into Paulina's limousine. "The hotel," she told the driver and turned to me. "What do you think of Gilda?"

I curled into her and mused for a moment before answering. "I think she's seen better days. She must have invested well, though. That villa is worth a fortune."

Her laugh was low, husky with a tinge of sarcasm. "She's an evil, decaying little woman who wants to appear "fated," like one of your American Tennessee Williams' women. Actually, she's a bitch more suited to DeSade. But she has her uses."

"Oh? What sort of uses?"

"How do you like sex?" Paulina ventured, moving in under my arm without an invitation.

"I think I'm fairly normal and healthy," I replied.

"That's a pity. You see, I'm quite peverted. Or haven't you heard of my reputation?"

I shrugged. "A little."

Now the laugh was lusty and loud. "Oh, you needn't be coy. My horrible reputation is one of the reasons I'm so much in demand for films."

She didn't get a chance to elaborate. We rocked to a halt in front of the hotel and I followed her into the lobby. I moved toward the desk for my key, but she held my arm.

"My key," I said.

"Aren't you coming up to my suite for a night-cap?"

"I didn't know I was invited."

"You're invited."

"Then I'm coming up to your suite."

"Then you won't need a key, will you?"

She was subtle, like a ticking time bomb with no numbers or hands on the face of its clock.

She had her key ready and ushered me quickly inside. As the door slammed shut, her arms wound around my neck. I could feel the warmth of her firm breasts against my chest. Her lips parted, poised and moist, ready for the kiss she expected.

"Do you always pick up strange men in strange bars?"

"You're hardly strange, darling," she chuckled. "And as for strange bars, I know the Casino lounge like my own hand. It's my only hunting ground when I'm in Monte Carlo. Now kiss me! You're sending hot flashes up and down my spine!"

"It's purely biological."

"It's the only science I know."

How, I don't know, but somehow she got even closer. Up on her toes, she arched toward me. Raising her chin, she brought her open lips solidly against mine.

Questions and angles ran through my mind, but her nearness drove them neatly away. She became an avalanche of grinding flesh, descending on me with reckless fury.

"Are you always like this?"

"Only with men," she intoned throatily and started in again.

The floodgates opened in a gushing frenzy as her tongue did its devastating work. My arms finally unlocked and went around her, pressing her tight. At last, when I could take her overwhelming onslaught no longer, I swooped her up and moved through the suite to the bedroom.

I deposited her on the bed, but she was on her feet in a second. Clothes went in every direction until only bare flesh remained.

She was built as I had never seen a woman built before. Her legs were unbelievably long and so perfectly shaped it seemed as if they had been sculpted. Her breasts jutted like a shelf of pink-tipped flesh, far from her chest with hardly any sag at all.

Her face, as she moved to me and her hands started undressing me, was a mask of heated passion. Her eyes were green, crystal clear, penetrating and cold, yet somehow charged with a heated sexuality that only enhanced the stunning beauty of the rest of her body.

When I was as bare as she, she stepped back and eyed me like a surveyor. Mediterranean moonlight flooded her body like a pool of liquid blue.

We fell to the bed with our bodies locked in the mortal struggle of passion. The heat of the room seemed to close in on us as we fought toward the climax. Our breathing strained and at times completely stopped as the tide of conflict reached its decisive end, exploding in our ears, anesthetizing our feverish bodies. I, and the stranger in my arms, became one for a split second of eternity, and when that eternity lapsed and reality returned, we lay in each other's arms so completely fulfilled that, by mutual consent, we agreed the fight was a draw.

I lay back smoking a cigarette while she quietly ran her fingers across the flat valley of her stomach. She barely moved, but just stared at the ceiling, lips cast in a wry, contented smile.

We hadn't talked all through our lovemaking. She chose to concentrate on the act itself and not the petty urgings and whispered pleadings so often encountered. Perhaps it was because we were, in essence, strangers to each other.

"Danger excites me." she said, at last, and rolled toward me. "You've an aura of it around you."

"You like to be around dangerous people?"

"Always," she replied, toying with the hair on my chest. "Why else would I agree to work for the French police and Interpol now and then?"

It was hot, sultry, the air barely moving, as I eased into a chair on the bay side patio of the Hotel De Paris and ordered a drink. The sun was just setting and the cooler evening air hadn't taken over from the heat of the day, a day I'd spent mostly in my own room.

I'd had to. The previous bedroom athletics had lasted until dawn. In conversation, between bouts of sexual gymnastics, I'd uncovered much of the enigma of Paulina Mendici.

She'd come out of the slums and poverty of postwar Rome some thirty years before. She'd been born to, and seemingly bred for, petty crime. It was for all expectations to be her way of life.

But the gangly teenager had developed into a voluptuous woman and been spotted by a producer of soft-core blue movies with a lot of nudity and no action. But the money was good, and it was a way up for Paulina.

That type of film was often the beginning, the middle and end of a career. But Mendici had something besides her body; she had talent. And, not only had she talent to act, she had the talent to choose the right people to sleep with.

In no time she was a success. Then scandal magazines and exploitive distributors got hold of her old films. For a while her career was in limbo. Thinking that her amoral previous life had probably ruined her, she threw caution to the winds and started living it for real.

It backfired. By gaining a scandalous reputation of a rather shady lady with little or no morals, Paulina Mendici became an even bigger star.

But she got bored. Years of living on the edge of disaster had given her a taste for danger and excitement. Her films gave her the money to do as she wished. So, years before, when Interpol had approached her for help in cracking an international drug conspiracy operating in the higher echelons of the European film community, La Mendici had jumped at the chance.

She'd worked for them, off and on, ever since. Her wealth, celebrity status, and reputation made her a natural to investigate Pastoria.

She'd spotted me through instinct, she'd said, and a natural inclination to bed down my "type." I pumped her to see how much she knew about "Nicholas Carr." As nearly as I could tell, she knew nothing. She did spot me as some kind of American agent, particularly since Interpol knew that there was one going into Pastoria.

"How exciting," she'd said. "Are you with the CIA?"

"No. I'm a clerk in the State Department, on special duty."

"I think that's bullshit," she had said, emphasizing the word as two words as in French. "But I think we should work together, nevertheless."

"I'm willing."

"Good. I'll make it easy to get you into the temple and, in exchange, you pass any unusual information on to me."

"Fair enough. When?"

"Tomorrow night."

At that point the more delightful part of our relationship again reared its beautiful head and lasted until dawn.

Paulina truly lived up to her reputation.

Now I had two women cohorts, both nonpros and both shaky concerning their allegiancy. Either of them could be a setup, but I figured anything they could give me was more than I had.

Cool lips hit my cheek and the area around the table became permeated with an all-too-familiar scent.

"Good evening, darling. Oh, isn't it exciting?"

She looked beautiful in a low-cut gown that accented yet left much to the imagination. Paulina eased her well-rounded bottom into the chair beside me and lazily swing her long, full-calved legs under the table.

The waiter arrived and properly gushed when she ordered a drink. He floated rather than walked away. Her voice just saying, "Pernod . . . merci," seemed to float on velvet strains of promised passion with every man she met.

"Do you affect everyone like that?"

"Only men, darling. Women hate me."

"I can see why." The waiter returned, placed her drink, took a longing look at her cleavage, and waddled away. "Are we set?"

"I had lunch with Gilda. During it, I used my shocked and gossipy voice and told her in strictest confidence that I'd been hearing rumors of a very wicked cult, discreet and exciting."

"And?"

"And a car is waiting in front, for both of us. Aren't you proud of me?"

"Very. Was Gilda shaky about me?"

"Only until I told her how rich you were. You build and sell tractors or something."

"Tractors?"

"Tractors are very expensive, darling. Shall we go?"

It was a cream-colored Bentley limousine, complete with bar and television in the back and a sullen, hard-eyed chauffeur in the front.

The car glided around the square in front of the Casino, made two turns, and headed north. In no time we had started to climb and soon left behind the tiny principality of Monaco.

I opened the cabinet in front of me. "Drink?"

"I could use one," Paulina replied.

Her hand was shaking slightly when she took the glass.

"Nervous?"

"Of course not," she beamed. "Just excited!"

I think she actually meant it.

The chauffeur pushed the limit and the big car

easily navigated the narrow, twisting mountain roads. We left the highway and the terrain became more desolate, with only a distant light now and then suggesting civilization.

Finally the road slanted straight up through an incredible growth of trees. Then we were through them and the road smoothed out and glimmered like a white ribbon before us. It led to a gate that opened electronically and closed with a whooshing sound behind us.

"You are in Pastoria," Paulina whispered.

She had barely finished speaking, when we rounded a long, banked curve and there before us was the Temple of Saabia.

"My God."

I nodded. "Impressive as hell, isn't it?"

In shape it was no more ominous than most of the castles dotting Germany and southern France. Until we got closer. Then the spiky towers, domes, rococo arches and tall, arched windows began to give off a nightmarish quality all their own. It was as if huge bats should be gliding from the windows. I looked up at the highest parapet, fully expecting to see their half-human master with his cloak draped open and his white fangs bared in the moonlight.

We pulled to a stop on a cement apron near a monstrous arch that appeared to lead into a lighted courtyard. The chauffeur padded around the car and opened the door. We oozed out, eyes working in every direction at once, and he motioned us toward the arch.

To our left and down the side of the mountain, I could see lights and, now and then, the hazy image of what appeared to be a long, low building among clusters of tents. I assumed that was Pastoria proper.

There was a huge, lighted door at the far end of the courtyard. It swung open just as we reached it and a huge, black man, dressed head to foot in black robes, filled the opening.

"Good evening. I am Gorn Motubu," he intoned, his voice like rolling thunder. "If you would follow me, please."

The way he said it left little choice. We stepped through the door, which was twice our height, and it whispered closed behind us—my first indication that the whole place was wired and electronically controlled.

We followed the black giant down an immense hall, evidently toward the temple proper. Incense, heavy, wafted around us and mingled with the scent from enough flowers to stock ten greenhouses. Brueghel, Goya, Spanger, and various cabalistic paintings vied for wall space with fourteenth-century drapes. The ceiling was muraled with something out of a Sorcery I text.

Paulina leaned close to my ear. "It looks like a set from one of Gilda's old movies."

"Or a high-class funeral parlor," I replied.

"Is he for real?" She motioned to the three-hundred-and-some-pound guide.

"Hormone shots. Shhh."

We stopped in front of a pair of huge, brass doors. Like the others, they had no knobs and seemed to glide open on the giant's breath. His bulk stepped from in front of us, and an equally tall man with a somewhat slighter build stepped forward.

"Mademoiselle Mendici . . . Monsieur, welcome to the temple of Saabia. I am brother Pierre La-Farge. Will you please follow me to the throne room?"

He was a tall man, powerfully built, with thick shoulders and a deep chest. Regal arrogance seeped through every expression and movement. He gave me the feeling of a man long accustomed to total control and absolute authority.

Paulina's arm quivered against my side as we followed him through a second set of monstrous doors. I wasn't sure the tremor I felt go through her body was out of fear or from anticipation of the spicy things to come.

The room was large, rectangular, and reeking of history. I could almost sense platters of food on long wooden tables and the yapping of mongrel dogs around them begging scraps from their medieval knights and masters.

But there were no tables. Instead there were large antique sofas and elaborate, high-backed chairs, all facing a red satin-covered throne at the room's far end. The throne was behind an equally large desk and under the only window.

Several other people had already arrived. They were clustered nervously in twos and threes, some sitting, some standing. I detected nearly as many languages as people from the low hum of conversation. Each of them seemed to be snatching wary glances at each other out of the corners of their eyes. Several eyebrows went up as we entered. In the eyes of those who knew her, La Mendici was obviously living up to her reputation.

"I think you've been recognized," I whispered.

"Of course I have, darling," she said, her lips

barely moving. "I'm famous."

"Do *you* recognize anyone?"

"A few. No one of any import."

LaFarge motioned us into one of the sofas and, with a stately bow, moved on through the room toward the throne. We were barely enveloped by the huge piece of furniture when a beautiful child-woman was at my elbow.

"Some aphrodesia, Monsieur?"

She shoved a tray of glasses under my nose. I looked at the murky, greenish liquid and then at her. She was much better, and a good indication of what was to come. If her body had been as transparent as the billowy monk's-type robe she wore, I could have seen the wall behind right through her.

"It will heighten the pleasures of the entertainment," she said, drawing my eyes up to her face.

She was young, with a smooth, clear complexion and sorrowful, full lips, sans makeup. But it was the thickly lashed, brown eyes that got me; there were hardly any pupils.

The girl was stoned out of her mind.

"I'll take a little heightening," Paulina said, lifting one of the long-stemmed glasses.

"Not I," I said.

"Are you sure?" Again the tray in my face.

"Quite sure. You've heightened me enough already."

The smile remained unmoved and the eyes stayed vague. It was as if she hadn't even heard the quip, let alone understood it.

She glided away, everything under the robe moving at once.

"You're old enough to be her father," Paulina

said, dipping her tongue into the green goo and frowning.

"That's what bothers me. I'd hate to see my daughter running around like that. Are you going to drink that stuff?"

"I was, until I tasted it."

"Ladies and Gentlemen. Good evening, and welcome to the Temple of Saabia. I regret to say, Count Drago will not be with us this evening. . . ."

LaFarge went on to inform us of Drago's current indisposition and do a pitch on the Temple and Pastoria. While he talked, I studied. I'd seen his picture, but it didn't do him justice. LaFarge, in person, was a striking character.

His hair was thick, with flecks of gray, and brushed straight back from a broad, flat forehead. The face was theatrically handsome, with heavy lips between a rounded moustache and a pointed beard. The eyes, under heavy brows, were coldly insolent. They seemed to penetrate every corner and every person in the room. His French was slightly accented and rolled from his throat as if he had just gotten the word from Hamlet, "Speak the speech, I pray thee. . . ."

That thought gave me ideas, and Paulina put a cap on them.

"I wonder why he just doesn't grow his own beard."

"You mean that one's a fake?"

"Of course. But a good one. He dyes his hair, too. No hair has a sheen like that naturally."

I slitted my eyes and focused in on LaFarge's face. She was right. The phony beard and the makeup were hard to detect, but they were there.

Mentally I stripped them and a few years away, and got a bingo.

Somewhere along the line, brother Pierre had been an actor. I'd seen him just the night before, in Gilda Morrow's film, as Count Dracula.

The man was a master of makeup, and that made me delve a bit further. I closed my eyes completely, listened to the powerful voice, and then reopened them to do some more facial rearranging, removing the beard and adding a scar.

There was no doubt about it. I'd seen LaFarge in another guise besides Dracula. I'd seen him on a horse, shouting orders and pumping bullets at a lifeless body in a tiny Andean village.

I was about to give the jackpot to Paulina, when LaFarge started winding down.

". . . and should any of you require privacy, you need but stand and one of our lovely young ladies will guide you to a room. And now, let the entertainment begin."

Suddenly he was moving, and half the wall—including the throne—was moving with him. It was a turntable, and when the 360 was completed, we were staring at a huge round bed on a raised dais. The wall behind it was covered with a rich brocade, and what wasn't brocade was mirrored.

The lights dimmed and the room was suddenly filled with a curious odor, a mixture of incense and flowers, like a Moroccan funeral parlor.

Then a mirror at the head of the bed slid aside and out stepped a young girl, stark naked. There were a few ahh's, a couple of ohhh's, and a lot of rustling as music filled the room and the girl started clumsily dancing on the bed.

"Whatever happened to good burlesque?"

"It went the way of the nickel phone call," Paulina whispered. "Shhh."

Two more nubile girls joined the first and the dance continued a la nymphs-in-the-woods. It was just getting hot and heavy, with the girls on the bed starting to paw each other, when two men and a woman down front stood up.

Instantly one of the girls was at their side and leading them toward the wall. The woman giggled as the girl ran her hand across part of the paneling and a door opened in the wall.

Then they were gone. Cute, I thought, real cute. The place is a gadgeteer's heaven.

A blond Adonis had joined the girls on the stage. They were working on his loin cloth when I took Paulina's elbow and pulled her to her feet.

"C'mon."

"Now? The show's just getting ... my God, look at him."

I looked, and felt very inferior.

"This way, please."

We followed the girl toward the wall. I had to tug Paulina all the way.

"Do we have to leave now?"

"I've got the urge," I replied.

"Oh, well, that's different."

Once through the panel, we followed the girl along a confusing maze of corridors lit with a green glow from unseen bulbs. Again the walls were draped in elaborate murals and tapestries of demons and saints.

"This place gives me the jeeters."

"I thought you liked kinky things."

"Kinky sex, darling, not spooky things."

Another wall number and we were in what could best be described as a thirteenth-century bedroom. The bed was a huge, ornate affair of blue and gold, with a plum-colored awning. Like the rest of the halls and room we'd seen, the walls were carved wood broken by expensive tapestries. Arranged around the room were tall pedestals holding gargoyle-shaped statues. They all pointed to the bed.

"Would you like me to join you?" The girl was reaching for the single button on her see-through robe.

Paulina coughed.

I sputtered but found my voice. "Uh . . . no, I don't think that will be necessary." She disappeared through the panel and I turned to Paulina.

She was smiling broadly. "You don't know what you missed, darling."

"Ah, but I only want you," I said, very loud, and pulled her into my arms. I ground my body against hers as lewdly as I could and pressed my lips to her ear. "Get over by the foot of the bed and take your clothes off. Make a production out of it!"

"You really do have an itch, don't you?"

"Not the kind you think. Move! And when you're ready, tell me to turn the lights out and join you."

Paulina did a much better dance of the seven veils than the girl on the bed had, and the end result was much sexier by the time she got down to the last remnants of underwear. But then Paulina had three times more equipment to work with than the three nymphs on the stage.

While she did her number I circulated from statue to statue, being careful to move low between
them. The third one was the charm. One of the
three gargoyles had an opaque eye. I was sure it
was one-way glass and it hid a camera. From the
curvature of the eye socket, I was pretty sure the
camera wouldn't have a much wider angle than the
bed itself.

But then, why should it? . . . the bed was all they
were interested in.

"Darling?"

I turned. There was no doubt about it. If anyone
was seeing the picture I was seeing, Paulina was
doing a good job of capturing their attention. She
lay on her back with her feet flat on the satin coverlet and her knees in the air. The knees were as
wide apart as they were high.

"Turn off the lights and come to bed, darling."

"Be right there." I added my best imitation of a
leering cackle and went to work on the panel behind the gargoyle containing the camera. When I
found what I wanted, I hit the lights and headed
for the bed.

"What the? . . ."

I silenced her with my mouth and pulled her
body hard against mine. After a long, cover-rus-
tling kiss I again found her ear with my lips.

"Groan!"

"What?"

"Groan!"

"But nothing's happening."

"Groan anyway . . . make believe you're in the
throes of lechery." She started groaning and throwing in an occasional whine and growl, while I ex-

plained. "There's a camera in the eye of one of the statues. I'm sure there's also a bug somewhere, probably in one of the bedposts. I don't have time to look for it, and I don't know if the camera is infrared."

She paused in the groaning and used my ear. "What's infrared?"

"Takes pictures." I rolled us both under the huge coverlet as I made a motion toward removing my clothes. Once there and hidden, I tugged one of the long, thick pillows down between us.

"What's this for?"

"That's me until I get back. Make love to it and keep groaning."

She took my hand and placed it between her legs. "I'm not that good an actress."

"Then manufacture the real thing," I said, and replaced my hand with hers.

I slipped from under the coverlet at the side of the bed and rolled under it. It was high and very long. I didn't think the camera could cover the floor at the foot of it.

At least I hoped it couldn't.

I started crawling in the pitch blackness as the bed above started shaking and Paulina vocally went into her act.

I smiled to myself. Either she was indeed one hell of an actress or she had taken my advice.

I found the catch on the bottom of the panel, heard a swishing sound, and scrambled through into an even darker void. Quickly I fumbled until I found a twin of the catch in the room and was rewarded with another swishing sound as the panel closed.

Cautiously, I stood and listened for any sound. My own breathing was the extent of it. A penlight from my pocket revealed a narrow catwalk just tall enough to take my height with a slight crouch. It ran both ways and seemed to go on forever.

Mentally, I flipped a coin and started left. As I moved I noticed that I was passing in and out of the incense-and-flowers odor. Also, thin slivers of light eked through panels that were slightly warped. It was soon clear that the catwalk I was on ran behind all the rooms, and could turn into a maze.

At a crossroads I fed Hugo into my hand and scratched an arrow pointing the way I had come. In the twists and turns beyond my light, there was a good chance I'd never find my way back to Paulina.

On I went, pausing to mark each turn with Hugo. It was like working my way through a house of mirrors, without the mirrors. Every time I passed a panel with sound on the other side, or saw a slit of light, it was accompanied by the whirring sound of a camera.

Then I felt—rather than saw—the floor start a downward slant beneath my feet. There was a slight draft on my face. I stopped, lit a match, and got my bearings from the direction the flame blew.

I came up against a panel twice the size of the others. My ear, against it, heard no sound beyond more whirring and an occasional click. I ran my hand around the frame and, click, the panel slid open. Blue, white, and gold lights flashed everywhere. A quick scan with the light told me that the room was jammed with computers, radio equipment, tape recorders, and video processing equipment.

I slipped through and found myself in a divorce detective's dream world. If it couldn't be video-taped, voicetaped, or filmed from the equipment in this room, it didn't exist.

One whole wall was stocked with video cassettes. They were all labeled with names, dates, and succinct descriptions of their contents. The names read like an international social register, and the descriptions would shock a pornographer.

I moved to a heavy steel desk in one corner and started popping drawer locks with Hugo. The contents of the biggest drawer yielded gold in the form of records.

Everything was there, entries of payments made by famous people into special bank accounts all over the world. It didn't take a trained eye or a calculator to quickly surmise that, page by page, I was unfolding a fortune.

Several of the names had red asterisks beside them and numbers done in a small, tight hand. The numbers were obviously a code that would yield me nothing without time to pore over them. There was, however, a pattern to the asterisks. They were all beside political figures and people close to heads of government around the world.

If these people were being blackmailed, I had a hunch it was for more than cold cash.

Footsteps and voices drifted through a door at the end of the room. Quickly I replaced the books and locked the drawers. I was at the panel, fumbling in the dark for the catch, when a key grated in the lock and the door started to open.

There was a curtain to my left. I didn't know what was behind it but it was the only place to go. I dived just as the room behind me was flooded with light.

CHAPTER SEVEN

LaFarge came through the door with Gilda Morrow waddling close behind him.

"It's crazy, I tell you," Gilda was angrily chirping. "And scary! And who's this Komand?"

"Never mind, Gilda," LaFarge replied. "The pictures should be ready in the darkroom. Stay here, I'll get them."

It was pretty clear, from LaFarge's direction, that I was in the darkroom. I moved to the side and whirled around. Enough light slanted through the curtain to survey the room.

There were shelves of bottles, two tables of developing trays, some furniture, and a large steel cabinet. I lurched toward it and yanked it open as quietly as possible. It thankfully contained nothing on the bottom of the shelves. I made myself fetal and crawled in, pulling the door behind me.

Light filtered through slots by my face. Gilda had followed LaFarge into the room. He was pulling eight-by-tens off a drier wheel and clothes-pinning them to a stretched wire while Gilda jabbered at his elbow.

"I don't get it, Pierre. We had a sweet deal . . . a little kinky show for the suckers, a little blackmail . . . why do you have to mess it up?"

"How do you think I'm messing it up, my dear?" He kept hanging pictures.

"Dammit, I know you are. All these hood types running around the place in those black robes. They got guns, I've seen them. When they came, our trouble started."

"They're security, Gilda."

"God, we're not the UN. Why the hell do we need an army for security?"

"I have my reasons." He hung the last picture. "Which ones, Gilda? Which of tonight's guests don't you know intimately or are not in your circle of perverted friends?"

"The ambassador said you didn't want money, Pierre. What the hell are you getting from him if it isn't money?" Her voice was quickly rising to a whine.

LaFarge turned and stared down into her fat, fearful face with eyes that glowed like two black embers of charcoal. "Forget the ambassador, Gilda. The pictures."

"Not until you tell me what's going on . . . who's this Komand? Pierre, he said if I didn't help him I'd have a very serious accident!"

"Gilda. . . ."

"No, Pierre. . . ."

LaFarge's hand was a blur, the smack of his palm on her face like the crack of a whip. With a cry she careened across the room and flattened with a thud against the wall. LaFarge was on her before she could puddle to the floor. One powerful hand folded around her neck and held her inches off the floor.

When he spoke this time, his voice was gutteral, raspy, and completely devoid of the cultured charm of before. I'd heard the pronunciation and accent many times in the gutter dives around the port of Marseille.

"Listen, you fat old pig, and listen well. When you and that idiot brought your petty little scheme to me I already had a going business. Between the religion kick and the side order of blackmail, my business has grown. Now this Komand wants in and I'm not letting him in, do you understand?"

He shook her until her head started a nodding motion.

"I still need Rudy, but you're hanging by a thread, Gilda. Now do as I say and look over the pictures!"

He released her, and Gilda wobbled toward the line of photos. I checked them. There must have been a camera hidden by the entrance door. The shots were all taken with people just entering.

"Her," Gilda croaked, pointing to a tall blonde on the arm of a distinguished older man. "And him, the boy with Countess Renfrow."

LaFarge snatched the pictures off the wire. "Is that all?"

Gilda moved on down the line and stopped at the last picture. "Him . . . the one with the Mendici whore. His name is Carr. I don't know him. She picked him up in the Casino bar last night."

"And you know nothing more about him?"

"Just that he's mean. He almost crippled one of my dear boys for life."

"Really?" LaFarge snatched our picture and frowned down at it.

"What business, Pierre?" Gilda was smiling now, the look of cunning returning to her eyes and the saccharine coyness creeping back into her voice. "Is it a profitable business, Pierre?"

He looked up, disgust spreading across his face. "Highly profitable, Gilda. In fact, so profitable and dangerous that knowledge of it would probably create an early grave for both you and Rudy. So I suggest you mention none of this to him."

She shrugged. "I can't mention anything to him, anymore. He'll hardly let me see him." She looked up with tears squeezing from the slits in her eyes. "It's over, isn't it, Pierre. I mean, Rudy really has flipped, hasn't he?"

"Let me worry about it, Gilda."

"That's why that phony seeress is here. Rudy thinks she really can get rid of his devils, doesn't he?"

"Rudy will last a while longer. Come along, I've got much to do." He took her arm, guiding her from the room.

"But what's going to happen to me, Pierre? I never bargained for all this. I just wanted a little money for my retirement."

"Just do as I say, Gilda, and nothing will. . . ."

Their voices were silenced by the slamming and locking of the door. I crawled out of my hole and pounded blood back into my legs until I could move without stumbling.

Once through the panel, I retraced my steps via

Hugo's arrows. Their conversation rolled around in my head as I moved.

Gilda had mentioned an ambassador being blackmailed for something other than money. My offhand guess was some kind of intelligence information. And it was obvious that Rudy Sturgis-Drago wasn't behind it and had no knowledge of whatever business was being run out of Pastoria by LaFarge.

There had been stark fear, unnatural fear, in Gilda's eyes when she'd been with LaFarge. I had a hunch she knew more about what was going on than she had even let on to him.

I slipped the panel away and was greeted with Paulina's voice, howling like a banshee, from the bed. Gently I dropped back into the room, slid the panel closed, and crawled back under the bed. The trip up under the coverlet was twice as hard as the escape had been. When I made it I was greeted with thrashing arms, legs and soft breasts.

"Is that you?"

"Of course it's me."

"God, where the hell have you been?"

"Checking secret passages."

"You idiot," she gasped. "Lord, I couldn't have lasted another ten seconds. Every muscle in my body aches and my throat feels like sandpaper."

I smiled to myself and filled my hand with one of her breasts. "Wanna fool around?"

"Are you kidding? I'm beat."

I slid partially out of my clothes and moved over her.

"Nick, I can't, I swear. I can't move!"

"You won't have to."

"Nick, I . . . oooh. . . ."

Two minutes later, Paulina was reestablishing her reputation, and groaning even louder while I established a new one.

The morning, outside my hotel window, was bright and the view across Monaco Bay and on into the Mediterranean was clear for miles. Several large yachts were bobbing in the center of the bay, with smaller craft buzzing around them like sycophant swans.

The message I'd picked up from the desk upon our return stated a noon conference with Serena at our previously appointed place.

It was nine now. That would give me time for a swim and some breakfast before setting out. I climbed into a suit, ordered breakfast, and made my way down to the lavish hotel pool.

It was already crowded with assorted types, sizes and shapes. There were tired German businessmen, bored American wives, and a rash of tourists made up mostly of leggy, bronzed ladies wearing only the bottoms of their bikinis and overly paunchy men who should have been wearing tops.

I did ten fast laps and pulled myself onto a chaise to dry off. A tall brunette a few feet to my right was giving me the once over. From the look I saw through my own slitted eyes, I knew she didn't have seduction on her mind.

She was gaping at the array of scars on my legs, one shoulder, and my side. It was the usual look I got when I took a swim in public places. I usually thought nothing of it. Scars, in my business, are almost welcome; they're healed wounds. If they hadn't become scars I wouldn't be there in the sun letting her gawk at me.

"Hello," I said, and smiled.

She nodded and tried to smile. It came out as a wan gulp.

"I'm an animal trainer in a circus. You know . . . whips, chairs and all that." I shrugged. "Sometimes I make a mistake."

Only then did she realize how hard she had been staring. She nodded again in embarrassment, and turned away.

"Mr. Carr . . . Mr. Nicholas Carr. . . ."

"Here."

"Telephone, sir."

He plugged it in. I ordered breakfast brought to my room and lifted the receiver. "Carr."

"Nick, this is your fellow debaucher."

Paulina's voice was sharp and clear, without a trace of fatigue. We'd arrived at the hotel, from Pastoria, around five that morning. The woman had marvelous recuperative powers.

"Good morning. Any word yet?" As we were driven away from Pastoria, we'd seen a long line of trucks weaving their way in on a lower, less-used road. They were marked Pyralee Construction. I'd thought that four in the morning was a strange time for them to be making a delivery.

Paulina had agreed, and we decided that her people—since Interpol and the local gendarmes would have more contacts—should do the checking.

"There is no such company," she said. "There was, about a year ago, but they went out of business. Bankruptcy. Most of the equipment was sold to an intercontinental mover called Sardis, Ltd."

"And Sardis?"

"They're all tied up in holding companies and parent companies and corporations. But Sardis seems to be mostly in freighters, ships."

"That figures."

"Nick, they're on my back for a report. It would help if you let me know something. After all, I am supposed to be investigating this, too."

I hadn't told her the full story of what I'd found the previous evening. She and her people were after a bunco, blackmail ring. If they thought they had proof, Interpol and the local law would be swarming over Pastoria like ants over honey.

I didn't want that. Not yet. I knew now we were onto something one hell of a lot bigger than blackmail, and I didn't want the big fish off the hook before they were landed.

"Stall 'em a little longer. I'll probably know something a little later this afternoon."

"I smell something," she sighed. "And the odor tells me I'm out of my league in this."

"Never deny your nose," I said with satisfaction. "Later."

"Wait, there's something else. You must have made quite a hit with Gilda on the ride back last night."

The old woman had moved in on us at the last minute, saying that her other guests had left without her. I didn't tell Paulina that I thought it was at LaFarge's command that she had gotten so chummy and pumped me the whole way back to the hotel.

"She's invited us to her chateau for a little dinner

party this evening. Just us. Gilda never has a dinner party for less than twenty."

"What time?"

"Her car is picking us up at eight."

"Cancel it. We'll take yours and I'll drive."

I hung up before she could reply, and took the stairs back to my room. Breakfast was waiting when I emerged from the shower. I had waded my way through three eggs, two rashers of bacon, three croissants, and was on my second cup of coffee when the desk rang up.

"Your tailor is here, *monsieur.*"

"Send him up!"

The "tailor" was Andre Monsanee. And I knew his visit was the result of a coded call the previous evening to Dupont Circle and AXE Probe. I'd never met Monsanee, but he had a fine reputation as a courier and as, what we call in the trade, an "obtainer." If you needed anything from an antitank gun to a dart pistol, Andre Monsanee could find it for you.

An effete little man in a dark, pin-striped suit flitted into the room. *"Monsieur, monsieur,* for you I will create a wardrobe of majesty!" His voice was high and cloying, and when he spoke the Daliesque moustache on his thin upper lip quivered. "There, put them there!" he chirped to two stooges loaded down with cloth samples. When they had, he snapped his fingers and imperiously shoved them from the room. When the door closed behind them, he turned to me and the whole facade melted away like so much makeup under cold cream. "Is the room clean?" I nodded. "Good, let's get down to it!"

The voice was brusk, an octave and a half lower, and the movements were extremely masculine and strident as he joined me on the wide couch.

"I never write anything down. I have total recall. Give me a few seconds."

He placed his well-manicured fingers at his temples, drooped his eyes, and seemed to float into some kind of a trance.

Ten seconds later he was facing me with open, clear eyes and speaking in clipped, staccato bursts of whole paragraphs.

"Your hunch was right. There was much more to Harvey Ames than we saw fit to uncover. It seems he had quite a theatrical flair and staged the early beginnings of Rudy Sturgis's cult. When he and Rudy had a falling out, it was because of ambition. Rudy didn't have enough for Harvey.

"Harvey assumed the name Carson, and made several second-rate pictures in Hollywood, working usually as a stuntman and technical advisor on special effects . . . usually explosives.

"The film you mentioned with Gilda Morrow was the only major role he had in the United States. Shortly after that, he disappeared and surfaced in Italy under the name of Zambisi. He again worked in the motion picture business and was suspected of running arms and stolen explosives into Cyprus.

"He was special-effects man on a film shot by a London production house in Ireland. While there, he was contacted by IRA terrorists and evidently went to work for them. He was arrested in London a year later and deported to Italy. Italy didn't want him when they discovered that his passport and papers as Zambisi had been forged.

"He mysteriously escaped while Italian authorities were trying to find out who he really was. The trail was blank for over a year, and then picked up in Algeria where he was up for hire as a mercenary.

"For the next five years he did everything from hired assassination to actual guerrilla fighting. He was captured in Zambia but purchased his release through a clandestine arms company in Amsterdam run by a man named. . . ."

"Komand." It was the first word I'd uttered since absorbing it all.

"Yes. Please don't interrupt. He became openly involved with Komand in an import-export business in the Netherlands. He dropped out of sight again, and as of this time we have no further data. As to an equation between the original Harvey Ames and your man LaFarge, we have no details or proof."

"I don't think there's much doubt about it. Coffee?"

He declined. "I was told to give you this."

He handed me a large ebony medallion trimmed in gold with a gold chain. "Fast work," I said, turning it over and over in my hands.

"My man worked all night. He's very competent. It works like this." He touched a hidden catch at the top of the chain and the dark stone flipped open. "The camera is infrared and the lens is of a very wide angle, so don't get too close to what you want to shoot. The shutter release is here."

The gold trim around the stone had six points, with tiny balls at their ends. He twisted one of the balls and I heard a faint click.

"You're preserved for posterity."

"Andre, you're a genius."

"I know. I'm paid to be."

"And the incendiaries?"

He reached in his briefcase and poured marbles into my hands. They were very much like my little bomb, Pierre, about the size of a thumb joint.

"They are timed. The white spots are treated for heat. Just hold your thumb over one, hard, for a few seconds and they're fused. Will ten be enough?"

"Plenty."

He stood. "Will there be anything else?"

"Not now. How can I reach you in case there is?"

He recited a number. "Repeat it back!"

I did and, before my eyes, the transformation was made back into the effete little tailor. As he skipped to the door I wondered which was the real Andre, and if there were any more.

The stooges gathered up the samples and then they were gone, leaving me sipping cold coffee and thinking.

If LaFarge was an explosive and munitions expert and had guerrilla and terrorist training, he'd gotten around a lot in the years since he was Harvey Ames. And that "gotten around" had made him a lot of contacts.

I was pretty sure I had it all now. The only question was what to do about it.

I remembered Serena and glanced at my watch. It was eleven-thirty.

"Another cup of tea, Mr. Carr?"

"No, thank you, *Madame*."

She poured one for herself. She must have been quite a woman in her day. Even past fifty, which she had to be, she was still beautiful. *Madame* Corinne Chevalier had run the biggest bordello along the Cote d'Azur for years. Then the free-lancers and the free lovers had moved in and the good madame retired.

But she hadn't retired her villa. Each of the rooms, or apartments as she preferred to call them, was available at any time, day or night, for an amorous rendezvous between already matched couples. Available, that is, for a price.

The villa was out of the way and the Madame was discreet. It was as good, or better, for my kind of meeting than a safe house. I'd used it a time or two in the past.

The price we had already agreed upon. The time was the next question.

"Will you and your wife be staying with us just the afternoon, or should I prepare?"

"I wish, Madame Corinne, that we could stay. Your hospitality is matchless and I know, from the past, that your cuisine is the same. But I'm afraid that both my . . . wife and myself have other engagements this evening."

"A pity. But I thank you for the compliment." She stood. The soft, clinging material of her dress rippled down her tall body, encasing the supple curves of, not an old madame, but a lush, mature woman.

"I'm sure that the maids have your apartment ready. If you'll follow me. . . ."

The study of following Madame Corinne's sinuous back and tautly muscled buttocks up a flight of stairs should become a part of every budding young man's curriculum. But since this was business, and I was far from budding or young, I checked around me for entrances and exits as we climbed, just in case. There were two, and easily accessible.

As I'd taxied down the coast, a nagging question had hammered in the back of my head. Why hadn't Komand and his group made a play for me in the time I'd been there? I'd screwed up his phony Serena and gotten the real one into Pastoria, but I was still on the outside and pretty fair game.

"Here we are." She extracted a key from her bag, unlocked a huge, high door and swung it open. Lithely, she stood aside and waved me in, a faint, expectant smile on her face as she awaited my reactions.

I reacted accordingly. In France, the pursuit of *amour* is an art and should be practiced in the proper surroundings.

The "apartment" had it all.

The living room, stretching to the front of the building on my left hand, was carpeted wall-to-wall with a shaggy off-white carpet thick enough to cushion any impact. From it around three walls sprung low couches in the same color, flanked by mirrors and sensuous shaded lamps that sprung into the "light to ravish by" at a touch of Corinne's hand on a switch near the door. The fourth wall was broken only by a door, ajar now at an angle that flung our images diagonally to the square of the other mirrors. By the edge of this door could be glimpsed a corner of a bedroom finished in flesh-pink, with again a multitude of mirrors in the same lustful tone reflecting a king-size round bed huge enough to contain the lust of a squad of Amazons. A scent of musky incense that matched *Madame* Corinne's heady odor further whirled my senses.

"Like it?" she asked, head tilted, tip of a rosy tongue just protruding from her full lips.

"Perfection," I said. "And I'm sure my lady will feel the same."

"I'll escort her up the moment she arrives. There is champagne on the side board."

She slipped out silently and I let down. It was nice, quiet, peaceful. The view through the huge windows was nearly as impressive as the apartment itself. From the villa down to the sea ran a wide, tree-lined esplanade with a maze of narrow, old-world streets running off from it in every direction.

I lit a cigarette and almost wished I were at *Madame* Corinne's for the same reason as her other customers.

And then the muscles in my shoulders tightened again as I saw her dark hair above the up-turned collar of a trench coat moving through the trees toward the villa.

"Are you sure you weren't followed?"

"Positive. I'm not a complete amateur at this, you know."

"Drink?"

"Yeah, but not that stuff." She nodded at the champagne. "God, this place should have been a whorehouse."

"It was, once. One of the classiest." I poured

Scotch, neat, into two glasses and turned to face her. She'd slipped out of the coat, and I saw why she'd been wearing it.

She was wearing some sort of playsuit-scanty halter-bra and a wisp of wrap-around skirt. She didn't look at all like a seeress.

"You've seen me in a lot less," she said, noting my look.

"I know, but sometimes more is better." I threw the drink down and let one of the huge chairs envelop me. "Talk to me!"

She sagged into a sofa across from me with a loud sigh and began. "He's a fruitcake. I mean, there's no doubt about it. It's as if he exists in a constant mood of depression. And he really does believe that Lucifer is dispatching a dark angel from Hell to come and get him."

"Did he buy your story?"

"Hell, he'll buy anything or anybody at this point, who might be able to get old Satan or Nickrobus off his back."

"Nickrobus?"

"Yeah. Nickrobus is the messenger that Satan is sending to get Drago. Don't ask me where he dug up "Nickrobus," because I couldn't find it in any of the occult books up there. And I mean this guy has a library on the black arts that won't quit!"

I was trying to figure how Nickrobus could fit into the scheme of things or could be used. My mind drifted away from what Serena was saying, then was yanked back, hard.

"What's that?"

"Huh?"

"What did you just say about a séance tonight to

summon Nickrobus?"

"That's how I got out of there today, along with my keeper, that monolith of an Indian—Gorn something-or-other. Drago is having his monthly big deal in the outdoor amphitheatre tomorrow. And tomorrow is very special. He calls it Pastoral Sabbath."

"What's that got to do with the séance tonight?"

"I'm getting to it. Can I have another one of these? I need it."

Reluctantly, I got her another drink and returned to my chair. "Go on!"

"He wants me to summon Nickrobus from the underworld."

"Oh, God."

"That's what I said. I can't summon a good belch without carbonated water. But, anyway, Drago wants to challenge this Nickrobus character to a duel of power tomorrow morning in front of his flock."

"He has flipped," I said, the beginnings of an idea filtering through.

"I know. So I got loose for a few hours so I could get some special junk for the séance. But this Gorn character came with me."

"How did you give him the slip?"

"He thinks I'm getting a massage. That's the only place I could think of where he couldn't follow me." She watched me think over the rim of her glass. "How'd you do?"

"How'd you know?"

"I saw you from my bedroom. It fronts on the parking area. Who was the old woman?"

"Not so old. She's a movie star."

"Rah, rah. Did you find out anything?"

I launched into it, starting with a rundown of who Brother LaFarge really was. That didn't interest her. When I got to the secret inner stairs running throughout the chateau, she perked up. When I got to the film and records room, she got absolutely ecstatic."

"Then they *do* exist!" She was almost rubbing her hands in glee.

I tried to remember when they had been mentioned before. I passed it over and went on. "But there's some kind of a code or key to them. It will take days and probably a good cryptographer to figure it all out. In any event we've got one hell of a lot more going on up there than blackmail."

I brought her up-to-date on my current theories and spread out a sketch I'd made of the chateau. "Okay, can you pencil in your room, the room where you'll have this séance, and anything else about the building that I've missed?"

She took the pencil from my hand and studied the drawing. "I don't know. They watched me like a true nonbeliever so I didn't get a chance to do too much moving around, but I'll try."

Her hand rapidly moved back and forth across the paper, and ten minutes later I flipped it around. "Good. More than enough. You've pretty well filled in what I couldn't get to." I pulled the locket and the incindiaries from my pockets and explained their function.

"Okay, now I'm a real spy. Now what do I do?"

"You're going to do the best hocus-pocus job you've ever done. You're going to produce Nickrobus."

She looked up and her eyes drilled into mine. She got it. Serena was a little dingy on most things, but now and then she caught on quick. "You?"

"Right."

"But how are you gonna get in?"

"You leave that up to me. Just make sure you insist on complete seclusion in that room tonight . . . no one but you and Drago."

"Easy enough, I think."

"And while I have a battle of wits with Drago, you slip through here." I indicated where I was sure a panel would be on the sketch. "And from there, here's how you get to the rooms with the records."

"And, once there, I photograph them all?"

"Right. Then set the incendiaries."

"And burn them up."

"You'll have whatever's important on film. The rest of it is of no use to us, anyway. And the fire will give us a diversion to get away."

I checked my watch. We'd been in the room a little under an hour. "That should do it. Let's go." I picked up her coat and held it for her.

Serena glanced at her own watch, up at me, then back at the watch. She seemed nervous, even confused.

"Something wrong?"

"What? Uh . . . yes, I guess so." Again the watch. "I . . . I guess I'm not too thrilled about hurrying back up there to that loony."

That was understandable, but I had things to do. "We've been here an hour."

"Fifty-six minutes." She took the coat from me and flung it across the back of the sofa. "How about another drink?''

"We. . . ."

"A wee one for the road? Please, Nick?"

I shrugged and poured two more glasses. When I handed her the glass she studied it.

"A little more, please?"

I figured she really was nervous. Back to the sideboard and back to her. We chatted inanely for about ten more minutes and I stood again.

She'd been stealing glances at her wrist so often during the conversation that I couldn't tell where her feelings were coming from. Did she want time to move along or to stand still?

She didn't speak until I again reached for her coat.

"Another one?"

"No way. You'll be so boozed up you won't find your way back to the masseuse and Motubu."

This time she let me slip the coat around her shoulders and take the glass from her hand.

"Nick?"

"Yeah?"

"Shouldn't we stay here a little longer? I mean, the old gal downstairs is gonna wonder. Don't two people usually take a little longer to . . . that is . . . I mean, hell, I always have . . . I think . . . I doubt if. . . ."

"You go out first. Just tell her that appearances are misleading. I wasn't all that I was cracked up to be." I was smiling now, trying to reassure her. She'd been rattling—or just rattled, it was hard to say—and that wouldn't do. For the part Serena had to play in this little escapade, she had to be cool, calm and collected.

I started maneuvering her toward the door.

"Nick, don't you think? . . ."

"No."

"But you ought to at least turn the bed down . . . mess it up a little."

"All right. Anything to make you happy."

I left her and moved into the mirrored inner sanctum. Carelessly, I took the playpen apart, throwing a pillow or two on the floor and half the expensively brocaded top covers.

"That's not a professionally done muss job."

I turned. She'd dropped the coat and was now standing, hip-shot, in the doorway. Her arms were crossed tightly under the halter, urging her breasts up over the top.

"I usually do it differently," I said.

"The sheets aren't even wrinkled."

She started moving toward me with a lot of body language. The change in her face was transparent, even if the reason for it wasn't. In London it had been hard. Since then, on the trip down and earlier that afternoon, it had been vacant. Now her features glowed with a very unSerenalike submissive sensuality.

"What about the other night, on the train?" I asked, recalling the rejection.

"I was getting around to it," she replied. "Besides, the situation's changed now."

"I don't think so."

"C'mon, Nick. Chalk it up to the liquor. It rearranges my hormones." Her hands reached outward, beckoning me to come to her.

I didn't move.

"What's the matter, Nick? Am I that hard to

take?" she quipped wryly, curling her fingers with inviting expectation. The tip of her tongue danced across the moist redness of her mouth as she arched forward, thrusting her breasts even farther out of the halter in my direction.

"Not now, love."

But Serena's about-face was for real. She wasn't about to take no for an answer.

Her arms went around my waist as she buried her face against my chest. "Mmmmm, I don't think you're that tired, Nick. Besides, you smell good."

"We don't have time." I didn't like the sound of my voice. It was growing weaker.

"We'll take time."

"Motubu's waiting."

"Let him wait. I take long massages." She giggled. "I have a lot to massage."

She proved it by moving it all against me. She was beginning to sound and feel more and more like La Mendici.

Her hands got under my shirt and then her nails were running up and down my back with long, enticing strokes. She pressed close, crushing her breasts flat, grinding her hips until her body seemed to melt against mine. Seething with desire, real or manufactured, her hands deftly moved over my body, exploring with knowing intimacy.

"Know what?" she purred.

"What?"

"It's hell trying to get anything done with clothes on."

The wrap-around skirt went first, and then everything underneath it. I kissed her again and matched her writhing and undulating.

Breaking the kiss, I studied her face. Her eyes were closed and her mouth was twisted with aroused desire. Removing the halter, I bent and used my lips on her pointed breasts. She sighed, pressing my head tighter against her.

"Nick . . . oh, Nick, you're reaching me!" she whispered.

I stopped all the action and stepped back. She was completely naked, except for her watch.

"That's what I'm supposed to do, isn't it?" I asked, grinning at her startled expression.

"What?" Her eyes blinked with bewilderment.

"Never mind." I shed my own clothes, led her to the bed, and joined her. I put my hands and lips back to work until she was whimpering and thrashing with mounting pleasure.

"Now! Now, Nick!"

We came together smoothly, our tensely moving bodies joining in a clinging embrace. I waited just long enough, and then went wild.

Our naked bodies sprawled across the bed in a tangle of arms and legs. Her velvety flesh slid wildly under me and then over me, moving and twisting, pushing us both to the edge.

Without warning, desire flamed into fiery bursts of pure ecstasy. We clung to each other weakly as the convulsive crest of passion swept through our bodies.

When I started to move away, she cried, "No, Nick! Please . . . again."

"Lord, woman."

"Please, please."

She started to move. There was nothing I could

do about it. She had a very persuasive body.

But, through it all, I could swear she was check-ing the time over my shoulder.

CHAPTER EIGHT

I climbed into the rented Porsche and wriggled my shoulders in the seat as I slid the key into the ignition. Just as I leaned back to twist it, a jabbing, needlelike pain hit my left side.

Poison needle. Stiletto. Dart.

They all went through my mind as I lurched forward and twisted in the seat to investigate. It was none of the above. It was a broken spring. And that was odd. The car was nearly new, less than five hundred on the odometer.

Porsche made better cars than that.

I opened the door to get more light inside and find a way to bend the sharp little piece of steel down. My eye fell on another piece of apparently faulty workmanship. About two inches of carpet had pulled away from the chrome slat running along the bottom of the door.

Gently, I eased the door closed as a sudden jolt of realization chilled my arms and my spine at the same time. I lifted my hand from the key and stud-

ied the wide, tree-lined street in front and behind
me. Other than a few pedestrians and a crowded
sidewalk in front of a cafe a few doors away, there
was nothing.

Should I do it here, or throw them off by throwing the little car into neutral, releasing the hand
brake and rolling down to the bay. It was downhill
and fairly steep. I was pretty sure I could make it
all the way to the boulevard that headed to my left
along the water.

Four or five long drags later, there was still nothing out of the ordinary along the street. I knocked
the ashes from my cigarette—as gently as though
their fall might cause a deadly blast—and started
to move. One or two pedestrians did a double take
at the car's silence, but no one else paid me any
attention. I hit the cross street at too healthy a clip
but there wasn't too much I could do about it.
Without the power to the brakes it took a lot of
man pressure and I didn't want to press too hard
against the seatback.

The turn made, I let the car roll to a stop by
itself, and let out a deep sigh. Swinging the door
open, I slid around into the rear seat and pulled the
door to behind me. Carefully, I ran my hand across
the upholstery of the driver's seat. It didn't take
long to find the longish lump toward the bottom,
just above and to the rear of where my butt had
been sitting.

I moved my hand some more. There it was; the
inside liner edge had been slit and restitched with a
clumsy, tack-style seam. Using Hugo, I cut the
threads again, stretched the seat liner up and ex-
posed the tightly bound sticks of dynamite the seat

contained. An electric cap was inserted into the end of one stick, and pale yellow plastic-covered wires disappeared under the seat, going towards the dash.

It wasn't a particularly good job, but then, they only had so much time.

Gingerly I skinned the insulation off both wires for four or five inches and wrapped them tightly together, deactivating the cap. Then I tugged it out of the slot in the dynamite, cut the wires on the engine side of my splice, laid the cap on the top cover, and extracted the now harmless bomb.

Weird images slid, then raced, through my mind. Just how would it have happened? Would the biggest force have gone up and the windshield withstood the shock? If so, I'd have been splattered in a misty layer all over the glass not unlike one of Dali's soggy humans.

LaFarge? I doubted it. The whole thing was a little too unsure for an explosive expert. And I guessed that anyone he would send from his squad of Untouchables would be as versed in blowing someone to hell as LaFarge himself was.

No, it was Komand. He'd finally decided to make a play for me. But why now?

I slid from the car and walked, with my deadly package, to the waist-high cement wall at the water. Another quick look around and then I tossed it as far as a gentle underhand throw would take it. It plopped in the water, paused, bobbing for a second, and then went under.

Back at the car I checked the trunk and then under the hood on the wild chance that they'd played it double, or even triple. Both places were clean.

I jammed my heel against the point of the offensive spring and settled back into the seat. There was still a little flutter in the middle of my guts as I turned the key, but it quickly went away as the motor roared into life and I got the car moving east toward Nice.

It took about two turns and five minutes to realize I was being followed. They must have, as I'd figured, left a backup or two in case I discovered their toy.

It was a big Bentley and the tailing driver was careful. He changed distances constantly, letting traffic intervene. I gained the Nice highway, went about four miles, and then turned up into the hills toward the old road. The Bentley made the same turn, but so did a big Army surplus ton-and-a-half and a little Volkswagon.

"Damn," I cursed to myself and the rolling countryside, "now who's who?"

They kept their distance all the way to the smaller road that ran parallel to the major highway all the way to Nice. I wondered when they would make their play, when the little Volkswagon came up on me, fast. I tensed as he got up beside me, getting ready for a little side-to-side confrontation.

It never came. There were two women, one very large dog, and a boy-child in the car. The kid waved at me. The dog barked at me. And away they sailed.

The big truck pulled about the same number and disappeared around a curve. The Bentley was still holding back, with the driver holding something to his mouth. I knew what when I saw a long radio antennae bobbing from the top of the boot.

I decided the best thing was to try and lose them on the curvy stretch of road I knew was coming up. I flattened my foot on the floorboard and leaned far back in the seat to lock my arms. The little car jolted ahead and I quickly gained ground on the bigger, less maneuverable Bentley. Trees, tiny farmhouses, and a small village with a fist-waving constable, sailed by. At the top of a rise I saw two tunnels and a long straightaway coming up.

Downhill plus the straightaway would give the Bentley an edge.

I tried to put my foot into the engine and urged every ounce of speed possible from the Porsche. I was just gaining daylight out of the first tunnel when I saw sunlight on the Bentley's chrome coming out of a curve and entering the darkness of the tunnel behind me.

I whirled around two sharp S-type curves and went hurtling into the second tunnel. It was about forty yards long and I was barely in the womb of its darkness when I knew something was wrong. The light was coming at me from the other end in a nice, round ball. I snapped on my lights and instantly saw why. The big, canvas-covered truck was stopped just inside the other end, blocking out most of the light.

I was about to do a little rear-ending. Just as I was slamming on my brakes and wildly fishtailing toward the truck's big ass end, I saw the Bentley creep into the tunnel behind me. If he didn't see the truck I'd be a small center between two very large bookends.

The tires screamed the last ten yards and I held my breath trying to make my brain compute what to do about the Bentley if I did get stopped. Then I remembered the horn and laid on it. That, of course, was futile if the truck was stalled. Then the sound of rending metal joined the horn to echo through the tunnel as the bed of the truck started peeling back the hood of the Porsche.

It stopped a foot from the windshield.

Quickly I checked the rear view for the bigger car. It had rolled to an easy stop about twenty yards behind. Movement from the canvas flap at the back of the truck caught my eye just about the time I figured out how the Bentley had been able to stop so easily.

They had known the truck was there. Just to the left of the bed, attached to one of the stakes holding the stretched canvas, was a twin to the long antennae on the Bentley.

Years of experience and a heightened instinct for survival saved my ass.

The roll flap on the back of the truck was going up fast, and behind loomed the fat snout of a 20 mm machine gun. I hit the driver's side door and flattened myself on the seat at the same time.

The machine gun started barking, sending shreds of glass from the windshield all over and around me. I felt, rather than saw, the backs of the two bucket seats being torn apart by the heavy slugs.

I counted on the darkness in the tunnel, and won. Sliding down my belly off the seat and behind the door, I waited until my knees hit concrete and then rolled like hell, pulling wide as I moved.

Six feet to the side of the car I came to rest on my belly, already sighting inches above the fiery spurts that were ripping hell out of the Porsche.

Two shots and the machine guns were silent.

I heard running feet behind me just as a second guy dived from the bed of the truck onto the hood of the Porsche. I weighed it all fast and decided that the pounding feet were closer and therefore more dangerous. Still holding Wilhelmina in both hands I swung around, hoping he was close enough.

He was.

I lashed out hard with the gun in a long, sweeping swing. He screamed as the front sight caught his face near the ear and laid the skin and flesh open clear across the right cheek. I heard the clatter of his gun fall on the cement and completed the 360 on around to the one on the hood of the Porsche.

He was teetering crazily as he tried to find some footing on the tiny bits of glass under the soles of his shoes. He did manage one shot that hit the side of the tunnel about a foot to the side of my head, spraying chips across my back and neck.

I took my time, aiming very carefully as he brought his .45 up for a second one. I squeezed off two slugs but only one was needed. The first one parted the bridge of his nose and he disappeared soundlessly on the other side of the Porsche.

I dropped to my knees and whirled back to the guy from the Bentley. He was uttering an endless stream of profanity as he used one hand to wipe the gushing blood from his face and the other to search for the weapon he'd dropped.

"Hold it or you're dead!"

A stream of cursing in German answered me and I heard the scrape of metal against concrete. I didn't wait for his hand to come up. I fired, point blank, six inches from the back of his head and he flattened like rolled dough.

I did a little cursing of my own for the next ten seconds. I didn't want to kill him. Just in case I would have liked to get out of him that Komand had engineered this. I preferred the actual fact of knowing rather than conjecture.

I was examining the cuts on my hands and judging the ones on my face, when I heard a sound from the far side of the truck. It was a click, barely audible, but there was no mistaking an opening door.

I quickly pulled off my shoes and soundlessly ran to the center of the truck. On my belly, I crawled halfway under and, in the gloom, saw a pair of size twelves vainly trying to tiptoe toward the Porsche.

I slithered the rest of the way across and then rolled. I must have made some sound I wasn't aware of, because suddenly the toes, instead of the heels of those shoes, were pointed my way. I was just bringing Wilhelmina up when one of them lashed out and my best girl skittered across the floor of the tunnel and collided against the wall.

I heard the swooshing sound of the blow that nearly took off my head. Then the blackjack bounced off my left shoulder and I went all the way down. I only knew that my whole side was strangely numb and that I was spinning like a pinwheel. My right arm was reaching out for him instinctively as my legs were trying to propel me upward.

I almost made it, when his foot caught me in the center of my chest and I went reeling again. I hit the ground and rolled into a ball as I heard him come after me. The spin didn't stop there; both sets of knuckles rasped the cement and the flailing blackjack missed my head by inches.

"You Basta, I get you, Basta!"

Not if I can do anything about it, Basta, I thought, rolling over painfully onto my back with my legs curled above me like two springs. I aimed my kick for his groin, but it landed in his guts. I knew it wouldn't stop him, so I rolled again. This time under the truck to regroup. The sharp, insistent throb in my bruised shoulder ran down into my paralyzed left arm.

By the time I emerged on the other side of the truck he was waiting for me, grinning and loping with his hands nearly hitting the ground like an ape.

"You dead," he hissed.

I'd thought of trying to take him down alive but, as a ray of light slanted across his face, I gave it up. There was no need. The faces of the already dead ones hadn't rung any bells. His face did. I recognized him as one of the two big moustached types I'd seen with Komand outside the pub john in London.

"No, friend," I said. "*You're* dead!"

He advanced deliberately this time, his grin widening and his eyes on my useless left arm. The blackjack was dwarfed in his huge fist. He menaced me with little tentative flicks of it as he approached.

It was dim as hell but I could feel the menace in his shadowed face, knew his eyes would be gloating on the features he fully intended to rearrange before finally ending it.

His arm was raised to bring the blackjack down when I flexed the muscle in my right forearm and tried to shake Hugo down. It didn't work. The chamois sheath must have gotten turned on my arm in the earlier part of the brawl. The spring release was either too low to let go or it was jammed.

I slammed myself against the truck as his arm came down. It went by about an inch in front of my nose. The force carried him by me and I helped out with a hard chop to the back of his thick neck.

It didn't even phase him. He stopped, got his center of balance back, and turned. This time I was waiting. The first one caught him high on the nose, the second sank into his neck at the esophagus, the third caught him on the jaw as he was already falling. I could feel the numbing pain from the impact clear up to my elbow.

He went down and spread like three hundred pounds of spilled sand. Quickly I assessed the situation. The tunnel was hopelessly blocked for the Bentley, the Porsche was a mess, and there was no way I could drive the truck down the major highway of southern France with the Porsche fastened to its ass without getting picked up.

I didn't have time to spend in the can or the means to answer a lot of questions.

I trotted into the sunlight on the Nice side of the tunnel and spotted nothing that resembled a house or other means of transportation. Hoof it? Eight miles to Nice? Hardly. My shoulder ached like hell and my legs and head felt worse.

I turned toward the sea. Less than a mile. Off I went.

I didn't stop to assess my damage until I was across the highway and scrambling down a hill to the beach itself, and felt reasonably far removed from the mess I'd made back in the tunnel. From the nearly two miles away I could still hear the blaring sirens and the honking horns of motorists not able to get through the carnage.

I looked myself over. The pants were in shreds and a little bloody from tiny cuts and scrapes along my legs. Likewise the shirt, only more bloody and in tatters. Blood was also dripping onto my shirt from my face. For the first time I was aware that something besides glass had gotten to me. There was a gash about three inches long in my left cheek. Generally I was a mess, and pretty sure I would cause quite a commotion among the general public.

The Med glittered a clear azure, with hardly any waves, in front of me. To my left was a small marina with a clubhouse and three piers jutting out from its various wings. To my right two fishermen were just pulling a small boat up onto the beach.

I headed for them.

"You want my clothes, my boots, *monsieur*?"

"That's right." I held out my hand full of franc notes and his eyebrows nearly reached his forehead. "You've had an accident, perhaps?"

"You might call it that," I replied, and urged an answer with a few more notes.

This brought a smile. "We can change in my house. It's not too far. Right up there."

His hand went toward the hills on the far side of the coast highway. It was in the general direction of the sirens and exactly where I didn't want to go.

"I've never known a Frenchman to be shy," I grinned, and added even more notes to the pile.

His smile was even broader and he started stripping.

The saltwater burned the hell out of my cuts, but I managed to clean most of the blood from my face and body before getting into his gear. He looked dumbfounded but pleased as he walked away in my tatters, jabbering about the good day's work and fine catch to his friend.

I walked down the beach to the marina and paused under the first pier. A few sunbathers lounged on the beach before the small clubhouse. None of them paid me very much mind. I scanned the other two piers and the immediate area of the tiny bay. All the boats were small, serviceable but not for what I had in mind.

And then I spotted it, a big twin-diesel powered job bobbing at anchor about a hundred yards out. It wasn't quite a converted minesweeper, but it was big enough and powerful enough to get me where I wanted.

I squinted my eyes and zeroed in on the afterdeck. It looked like a party, and it looked like it was just breaking up. I climbed up onto the pier and moved up some wide steps to the marina clubhouse. There was a pay phone just before the door leading into the lounge. I stopped there and gathered coins enough for the call from what the fisherman had left in his pants.

I had more than enough to reach Monaco and the Hotel de Paris.

"Nick, where the hell have you been? I've been trying to get you all afternoon."

"Moving just as fast as I can," I replied. "Listen, there might be some trouble." I didn't add that there already had been. "I want you to pack and get out of there."

"Where shall I go?"

"We have a dinner party at Gilda's, don't we? I'll meet you there. We won't be properly attired and we'll be early, but I don't think the old lady will have any complaints."

"All right."

"There's more. Take your own car to start with, but dump it fast." I went on to explain in detail how to spot and get rid of a tail.

"Is that all?"

"No. Get a pencil." She left the phone. When she returned I gave her Andre Monsanee's number and a long list of what I'd need for the coming evening.

"Good lord, are you going to start World War III or make a movie?"

"Maybe a little of both," I chuckled. "Have you got everything? It has to be exact."

"I think so." She read it back to me.

"Good girl. See you in a couple of hours."

"Nick?"

"Yeah?"

"There's more to this than I was told, isn't there."

"Yeah, baby. One hell of a lot more."

"I'm scared."

"Too scared?"

"Yes, but I'm a good actress, remember?"

She rang off and I turned back to the boat. There were still a lot of people milling around on the afterdeck and a small powerboat was ferrying them into the pier by fours. I estimated another half hour and figured that out in the open, where I was, wasn't a good place to wait.

I was on a patio, and through the glass doors I could see another glass wall and patio in front leading to a parking lot. Perfect. From the bar I had a good shot at anyone entering from either side.

I felt a little conscious of my wardrobe, but subtly overcame pride as I pulled the dark cap as low as possible over my eyes and entered.

I took one of the high, comfortable stools at the clubroom end of the nearly deserted bar and ordered beer when the bartender arrived. He compressed his lips as he looked over my clothes and then closely into my mangled face.

"Beer," I repeated, and moved two twenty-franc notes across the bar. "Keep the change."

His scrutiny disappeared along with the twenties and I had a cold German lager foaming in front of me.

I felt a little prickle run up my spine, and swiveled my head around the room.

A rotund little man, who had *mein host* written all over his pendulous jowls, was regarding me with a most pleading, anxious expression. It said, "you can't be a tourist, you can't be a member, who can you be?" His eyes were black pinpoints in that screwed up gaze until I waved and pointed to the big pleasure craft bobbing in the bay.

I don't know what I meant and I don't know what he thought, but his gaze wavered and I suddenly got his professional cordial smile. Whoever owned the boat must have been a good customer. I turned back to my beer.

Then I noticed the quiet. The few people already in the bar weren't talking. The four men playing cards in the corner weren't playing. It was as if everyone were waiting for something to happen. Without lifting my head I rolled my eyes around to the various faces. They were filled with tension and suddenly I knew something was dead wrong. Everyone in the place that I could see, including the two men talking in low tones at the other end of the bar, had been giving me covert glances before I'd ever thought of giving them any.

I felt my hackles rising as my usual, danger-warning sensory impression tried to get through to my active mind.

Then I got it, something that had tried to register ever since I had come into the room. Silence. Outside there was laughter and gaiety, but inside was a morgue.

I was swiveled halfway round on the stool and had one foot on the floor when they walked in; Komand and three of his stooges. They walked through the kitchen door and I could see another of their kind behind them, a Luger trained on the kitchen staff.

His boys had blown it, so the big man himself had decided to join the fray. They had probably covered the highway for a few miles both ways and discovered I hadn't gone that way. Straight up into the hills and inland France was out. The sea, and right where I was, was the only place I could be.

I heard no shots and, from a glance in the mirror, saw no movement toward me. Yet.

"You two," the voice was low, but the rusty

tones that I knew only too well had the Komand power of command about them. "You move on down next to the one at the other end of the bar . . . the one in the boots."

I stole a look out of the corner of my eye to see what the customers would make of that. They were moving toward me meekly enough, but it flashed over me that these two weren't customers. They had the swagger—cowed as they were trying to make themselves—of professional strong arms.

I began to realize that my act of innocent customer had already checked out phony as hell. I got the picture. Komand's little army had already raised enough hell for one day. He didn't mind taking the place over by seige, but he didn't want any more killing, at least not in front of a whole beach full of people.

He wanted to get me out of there before taking me apart.

Beyond Komand, *mein host's* round face had dissolved into a mass of shapeless dough in which his buttonlike mouth quivered with the effort to speak. His hands kept massaging each other until in his anxiety he danced forward, fluttering them toward Komand.

"But . . . you can't! . . ."

Komand pushed him gently to the side, effectively silencing him, as he and the two behind him started my way. The other two were less than five feet away now and obviously tensing for their move.

I moved my right arm slightly forward and, with my left hand, gathered in a salt shaker from the bartop. With my thumb and index finger I unscrewed the cap and dumped the contents into my fist. They were just reaching for me when I showered both their faces. They backed off much faster than they'd come and I grabbed the heavy beer stein as I whirled and leaped from the stool.

"Look out . . . IT IS HIM!" Komand cried. Then his face disappeared in a welter of broken glass and beer as I swung toward him and body-blocked the other two in a simultaneous reflex action.

I got one and missed the other. He came back fast, swinging the butt of a Walther he'd pulled from under his coat. I could only partially dodge it. The blow, aimed at my head, glanced off my jaw, but still had the power to stun.

My legs nearly failed me. Then somehow, blindly, instinctively, I had him gripped by the throat and the crotch, my head buried in his shoulder. I hung on until my senses cleared, taking his feeble blows on my back from the Walther.

The two salt victims had recovered enough to find me with their red-rimmed eyes and were on their way. I picked up the one I had like a sack of feathers and threw him squarely into their faces as they dived for me.

I had started my turn toward the kitchen, then remembered the one already there, with the already drawn gun. Surely by now he would be forewarned. I veered off and ran through the wide doors into the dining room. In the heavy boots I clomped, plunged, and stumbled through tables full of wide-eyed diners.

I jumped a buffet table at the end of the room and went right on through two closed French windows. Outside I rolled clear across the porch and over the sand. I came up clawing at the boots and running again when they were off.

I still figured the boat to be my only chance, but didn't have the vaguest idea how I was going to get out there. If I veered off and headed for the water, I knew I could swim that far, but they'd nail me easy every time I came up for air. They hadn't started firing yet, but the temptation of a sitting duck in the bay would be too much to resist.

I scrambled up an outcropping of rocks and dropped to the sand on the other side.

The solution to my problem was five feet in front of me. A young guy was shaking out a wet suit he'd obviously just crawled out of. On the sand by his feet lay a snorkel and a pair of fins.

I clawed all the remaining bills from my wallet and waved them in his face. "I want to buy your suit and the fins."

"Not for sale."

I don't usually involve the general citizenry, but in this guy's case—and soon the captain of the boat in the bay—I had no choice.

I was careful not to break his jaw when I hit him and caught him as he fell. I laid him gently in the sand and stuffed the money down his trunks.

I gathered my loot and put four more sets of rocks between myself and the marina before tearing off my clothes and pulling on the wet suit. Wilhelmina went next to my belly where she could stay dry, and Hugo went between my teeth, just in case.

The sun was dipping fast. I knew I would be a mere shadow against the waves but I stayed under, using the snorkel, most of the way anyhow. Swimming was tough. Because of the numbness still in my left arm, I had to rely on the fins.

By the time I'd surfaced on the seaward side of the boat, I felt dead from the hips down.

I listened. There was no sign of anyone left from the party as I kicked off the fins and mounted the aft ladder. A young girl in her teens stood at the rail. She faced away from me, watching the chaos ashore, but turned when I hoisted myself over the rail. My weight was just enough to make the boat roll.

She opened her mouth to scream just as I reached her and closed it off. I had her around the waist, one hand clapped across her mouth. I could feel her spittle running between my fingers as she kept on trying to scream through my hand. She clawed at my neck above the rubber of the wet suit. At the same time, her sharp toes in a pair of pointy slippers raised hell with my ankles as I half-dragged, half-carried her toward the wheelhouse.

By the ladder leading up to the wheelhouse and the companionway leading down to the cabin, I twisted her around until I could get both of her hands in one of mine. I also got part of the ladder between us so she couldn't kick me anymore.

She was a wee one, but she was a tiger. I listened for a moment, hoping our scuffle hadn't been heard from below. Nothing.

When I realized that she was choking for breath with my hand over her mouth, I released it a little. I didn't take it away entirely.

"Listen," I whispered in her ear, "I'm not going to harm you. I just need a ride, a loan of your boat for a couple of hours."

She seemed to relax a little, and I made the mistake of releasing her. Again her mouth opened to scream, her chest expanded frantically to really cut loose. I grabbed her just in time, and gave her a good shake in exasperation.

"Dammit, listen to me! I'm not going to harm anyone. Now how many others are there on the boat? Hold up your fingers!"

Tentatively she raised her hand and one finger.

"Man or woman? Man, nod."

She nodded.

"I'm going to let you loose now. Call him up here and I promise you nothing will happen to him or you."

I took my hand from her mouth and gently eased her around to face me. When I was sure another scream wasn't forthcoming, I pulled the snorkel off and tried to smile through the salt-burning cuts.

"You aren't going to rape me?" She said it as if she were disappointed.

"No, not today."

"Are you a sea pirate?"

That I had no answer for. "Will you call your friend, please."

"Antoine . . . Antoine, there's someone here to see you."

A tall, stately, and very drunk Antoine staggered up the ladder and leaned against the rail. He brandished a bottle of champagne in one hand and two half-full glasses in the other. "I thought all the guests had left, my dear."

"I'm not exactly a guest, sir. But I'd like to be for an hour or so. I need a ride around the point, to a villa landing about halfway between Monaco bay and Nice."

His eyes seemed to glaze even more with the effort of assimilating what I said. "We really weren't going that way, old boy. I'd thought of going the other way, as a matter of fact . . . over to St. Tropez. Why don't you join us? Be a smashing party."

"He's a sea pirate, Antoine," the girl said. "He doesn't want to go to a smashing party . . . and he doesn't want to rape me."

"Really? What do you want, old boy?"

"I told you, I . . ." I started to explain, and even invent a story, but decided I didn't have the time. "Look, I'm a desperate criminal. I've just robbed a casino in Cannes and I'm trying to get away. I've got a helicopter waiting. I'm willing to pay. . . ."

"Pay? Nonsense. Why didn't you say so in the first place, old boy. Those bastards have taken enough of my money. Glad to see someone bugger them up for a change."

"Then I can use the boat?"

"Absolutely," he said, swaying slightly again. "Afraid you'll have to drive it yourself, though. As you can see, I'm not in the best of shape . . . as a matter of fact."

I started up the ladder to the wheelhouse and paused. "Do I have to tie you up?"

"Tie us up? Absolutely not. How in the world can I drink with my hands tied?"

He headed back down to the lounge as I climbed the ladder to the cockpit. I snapped the governor on the port generator to "Start," hit the switch, and was answered by a throbbing pulse. Oil pressure and cooling flow were adequate. I gunned the starter engine up to speed, kicked in a panel circuit breaker that flooded the boat with bright lights, shut off the battery light circuit, and cranked the pair of big diesels that furnished propulsion. Everything on the instrument panels checked right and the tanks said full.

I headed out and soon threaded my way through the tricky channel turn, picked out the sea marker with my spotlight, and shoved the throttles to cruise power. The boat accelerated smoothly, its phosphorescent wake creaming behind it, a bow wave, crisp and sharp, veed out at the sheer. When I rounded a bend of land and made open sea I searched and found the autopilot. Snapping it on, I stepped back and checked.

Sure enough, the big wheel spun back and forth mystically, as the gyroscope held the boat truer on course than would a human pilot.

I heard grunts and groans coming from the ladder. With my hand on Wilhelmina's butt under the wet suit, I stepped from the wheelhouse in time to see Antoine, with a huge round tray, come over the top.

"Thought you might like a little liquid refreshment, old boy. Nothing like it on a moonlight cruise."

CHAPTER NINE

With a wave, and an answering smile from the precocious woman-child, I slipped into the sea. Antoine had passed out halfway through the trip, so I'd checked her out on the boat so they could make it back to St. Tropez. She'd proved to be already versed with most of its workings because Antoine passed out a lot in their travels.

As I'd instructed, she waited until the boat drifted clear of my bobbing body, then revved the diesels. She moved away softly, then veered in a wide arc and turned back from whence we'd come.

I turned my attention on the villa. It sat on a ridge a good hundred yards above the sea. Well-landscaped gardens and a winding walkway led up to it from a short pier.

On my previous visit, every light in the place had been on and I'd seen it only from the front. Against the background of the sea and the clear, far horizon that night, it had taken on the traditional romantic splendor of the Riviera.

Tonight, particularly from my vantage point— bobbing in the sea—it had an ominous quality. Only two rooms were lit, and those very dimly. The villa itself was starkly outlined against a smoky sky.

I sniffed the air and smelled a storm. Around me, waves were already starting to create bigger troughs. Well, I thought, if Paulina comes through with what I want, a little rain and a lot of clouds will be just what Doctor Carter ordered. Before long I was working my way through crashing breakers and the foaming water was getting shallow enough to walk through.

I surveyed the beach in both directions. On my right I could see the glow of Monaco above the hills. On my far, far left, a larger glow that would be Nice. The lights in the villa were about a half-mile distant, toward Nice. I got to my feet and trotted toward them. As I got closer I realized how secluded Gilda's place was. Hers were the only lights for nearly a half mile on either side of the villa.

LaFarge paid her well, I mused. That big an estate on the Med coast was pure gold.

I barely climbed the ridge and reached flat land when the rocks and high growth became the well-manicured lawns of Gilda Morrow's estate. I cut my pace but kept at a trot as I moved from tree to tree toward the house.

It took me nearly twenty minutes to completely circle the place. There was no sound anywhere, and the only lights were in two sets of windows on the second floor.

Obviously there wasn't going to be a big production made of our dinner party. I didn't see a servant anywhere.

Paulina was late . . . not much, but enough to worry me.

I made my way down the long drive to the huge, steel gate. It gaped open. There was no sign of a car, empty or occupied, for over a hundred yards on down the narrow lane.

I decided not to wait, and returned to the house. High, French windows opened easily under Hugo's point, and I moved through a huge, book-lined study and into the great hall. Still the only light came from apparently open doors somewhere in the upper hall. It was dim but enough to mount the side, curving staircase.

I replaced Hugo and fished Wilhelmina from under the wet suit as I moved down the hall. The first lighted room was the screening room where we had seen Gilda's horror flick. It was empty now, and chaotic. Whoever had searched it had been thorough, right down to dismantling the wooden panels and ripping the brocaded paper from the walls.

Back in the hall, I moved toward the only other light. I was just nearing the door when I heard the low, whining sounds. It was unmistakable. Gilda's two poodles.

I remembered how they had barked and raised hell at the entrance of every guest the previous evening. Surely they could both hear and smell me approach. Why didn't they bark now? I eased Wilhelmina's safety off, crouched with my back against the wall, and rolled into the room.

I saw why the dogs weren't barking. One was

sitting at Gilda's feet, licking her ankles. The other
was in her lap nuzzling her hand, wanting to be
petted.

They would never be petted by Gilda again. She
sat, immobile, eyes open, staring straight ahead. If
the eyes didn't tell me, the raw, red marks on her
throat—four fingers one one side and a thumb on
the other—said it all.

Gilda Morrow had been put to sleep for good.

I only hoped that whatever she wanted to tell me
hadn't died with her. Her bedroom, like the screening room, was a mess, carefully torn apart. It didn't
take me long to find out that they had gotten whatever they were looking for.

One of the two desks in the room, a massive antique Louis Quinze, had been pulled away from the
wall and the back ripped out of it. The contents
were spread across the carpet, but I was pretty sure
that Gilda's killer or killers had gone through every
item there and taken just what they needed. I was
also pretty sure that it had been the woman's
sucker list, her version of the guests to the Temple
who had been blackmailed.

The rest of the room offered nothing and I was
about to give up, when something hit me. Only a
third of the room had been ripped apart, and that
only in the general area of the antique desk.

The bed, its stands, a sofa-tea table combination,
and a second desk hadn't been touched. They'd
gotten everything they wanted from the back com-
partment of the antique.

I noticed the disarray on the newer desk across
the room and figured that Gilda had been doing
something there when surprised. The chair she was

sitting in, and died in, was obviously the mate to that desk.

I went through the drawers quickly. Nothing but the usual: stationary, pens, pencils, odds and ends. The top was different. Gilda had been doodling on several scratch pads and the results were strewn all across the desk top. There were three books on heavy armament and munitions and one on modern aircraft opened, and marginal notes had been made beside specifications.

Little things started to click in my head. Gilda Morrow had been much more cunning and bright than she had let on to the world. There could be only one reason why a faded ex-movie star turned blackmailer would be interested in the size of a tank or weapons carrier.

A slip of paper extended an inch or two from under the desk blotter. I pulled and kept pulling. It was a topographical map of the area. I threw the blotter to the floor and found two more maps under it. Both were sectional blowups from the larger original. It didn't take long to figure out that they concerned the immediate area in and around Pastoria.

Gilda had also made notes all over these. They were cryptic and generally illegible, but her interest seemed to be centered around one circled area.

From a drawer I got a magnifying glass and started deciphering her scrawling hand. In her own way, Gilda had carefully laid out the Temple, the buildings in the valley of Pastoria itself, and the area of the outdoor amphitheatre where Drago held his Pastoral Sabbath sermons.

This was the part of the map Gilda had circled

and seemed to concentrate on. There were tiny dots all over it, as if she had been driving her pencil down again and again at the paper.

In triumph? It had to be. And chances are she, thinking I was in with Komand, was going to tell me what she'd found in exchange for money and/or a piece of the action.

Back and forth I moved the glass, until I found a double underlined notation: "Pardeaux—pp 168 –9."

I flipped back through the stack of books on the table until I found it: "Emile Pardeux, *Caves of Southern France.*" The two pages made up another map, an underground map.

I ripped them out and carefully placed them over the sectional map. One area was dominated by a huge underground cavern. I lightly traced it out and then lifted the map from the book from the one notated by Gilda.

It didn't take an experienced spelunker to figure out that the cave or cavern was located right under the outdoor amphitheatre.

I was rolling the maps up when I heard a gentle footstep in the hall outside the room. Quickly I grabbed a mirror from the desk drawer and slipped to the floor. On my knees, I slowly moved my hand holding the mirror into the hall. I saw the feet first and then the lower body. When the mirror tilted up, I sighed and relaxed my death grip on Wilhelmina.

With her eyes wide with fear and caution, Paulina was tiptoeing down the hall as best she could on six-inch heels.

"Stay right there, Paulina. I'll be out in a second."

There was an "Eeek!" and then a "Nick?"

"Yes. Go back down! I'll meet you in the lower hallway."

I scurried back to the desk, carefully folded the maps, and stored them against my chest under the wet suit.

"Oh, my God."

I whirled. Paulina was standing in the doorway, staring, with her hands flat against the side of her face.

"I told you not to come in."

"Is . . . is she? . . ."

"Very." I hustled her into the hall and down the stairs. "Where's the car?"

"About a hundred yards down the road . . . in the driveout, just where you said."

"Did you pass anybody on the way from the highway?"

"No. Who killed her?"

"I'd guess LaFarge or one of his Untouchables."

"But why? I thought they were all in this together."

"They were. But only part of it together. C'mon, I'll explain while you drive."

We climbed up and away from Nice and the ocean. In no time we were swallowed by the trees and shifting direction to skirt the hills that would soon become part of the Pastoria preserve.

Paulina drove while I changed clothes and assembled all the gear and paraphernalia she had amassed for me from Andre. He was truly amazing. Everything I'd asked for, down to the red sash around my waist and the soft rubber mask with a mane of long black hair, he'd been able to give

Paulina in the space of a few hours.

"You look like something out of a Dracula movie . . . or worse," she said, one eye on the rear-view watching me crawl into the black frock coat.

"Just so I look like I just crawled up from somewhere in the vicinity of hell."

There was a long pause as she drove on the narrow road. Off to the left and far below us, I saw the blinking lights of what I hoped was Pastoria. If my calculations were correct, we would end up on a minimountain directly above and across from Drago's Temple and the amphitheatre beyond it.

Paulina's voice, when she spoke again, had an edge of seriousness in it. "Are you going to tell me what this is all about now?"

"Why not. My theory is this: LaFarge's real name is Harvey Ames. Without going into a lot of detail, I'll summarize it. He and Komand were in an arms smuggling-and-selling business. But it wasn't growing fast enough for LaFarge. So, when Gilda and Drago came to him with their deal about the religion rip-off and blackmail scheme, LaFarge saw a way to broaden his base of profits and launder the money from his arms sales.

"His idea had been to *start* revolutions, rather than wait for them to start. Komand had vetoed it, but after it had been successful a few times, he wanted back in. That's when LaFarge expanded his army of Untouchables in Pastoria."

"And Drago didn't know all this was going on?"

"No. Watch the road!"

"But Gilda figured it out?"

"Yes. She probably wanted to make a deal with Komand through me. I'm pretty sure she thought you and I had something to do with Komand. She was going to sell me her list of suckers tonight, but LaFarge got to her first. She must have reasoned, or been told by one of her own contacts, that La-Farge was blackmailing certain political figures, not for money, but for help in starting revolutions in their own countries.

"And then LaFarge would sell them the arms to keep their private wars going?"

"Exactly," I said. "I got the tip-off on LaFarge when I found out he was an actor and a master of makeup and disguise. I saw him get one of his revolutions started in South America a few weeks ago. Only then he looked a lot different and had a scar clear across his cheek."

She slid around a curve, righted the car, and shifted down for the last steep climb. "But why do you have to go back in there? Why don't we just call out the police and the army?"

"Because I can't let that list of LaFarge's contacts fall into the wrong hands, and I can't chance LaFarge getting away."

Our eyes met in the mirror. "You're going to kill him, aren't you?"

I nodded. "I'll probably have to. Pull over here!"

The car had barely stopped before I was out the back door and dragging all the equipment behind me. It took nearly twenty minutes to put all the pieces of the hang glider together and tie all the extra bags and belts of what I would need onto the rail.

"You're really going to glide all the way over there?"

I followed her gaze. About eight miles away I could see the fuzzy outline of the Temple against the dark sky. Between me and it there were the lights of a few farmhouses, another castle, and a lot of trees. I hoped there would also be a lot of up-drafts coming in from the ocean to the south.

"It should be simple from this height," I said, buckling the glider's straps to my body. "Ready."

I hoisted the glider until the rail was about crotch high and backed off about fifteen yards from the edge of the cliff. She followed and stood directly in front of me.

"I think you're crazy."

"Have to be a little crazy," I grinned, "in my business."

"What is your business, Nick?"

I studied her face. Her lower lip was quivering as she took it between her teeth and bit down hard. She was very beautiful, standing there drenched in moonlight with the faint breeze blowing her long, silky hair around her straight shoulders. Very beautiful, and very out of place.

"You don't want to know, Paulina."

"You're more than just a lacky of the State Department, aren't you?"

"Go back down, Paulina. And if you don't hear from me by tomorrow noon go to Andre and tell him everything I've told you. Tell Andre first, and then you can tell your own people."

She kissed me, long and hard. The breeze was warm, like the night around us, but her lips were cold.

Then she stepped aside and I started running. I hit the edge solid with both feet and threw myself out into space. A little bile came up into my throat as the glider caught, faltered, and then fell like a rock toward the bottomless, inky blackness below.

I leaned forward and pulled the glider's tail down with the ankle lines. My speed increased, but I couldn't catch a current. On down I went until I was sure there was no sky left as the darkness of the trees rushed up to greet me.

Then I felt it, a rush of warm air on my face. I felt the lift and adjusted my body to take advantage. Then I was lifting. I caught another, stronger current and began to soar.

When I was sure I had the altitude, I swiveled my head around and saw her, still standing on the cliff with her hands to her eyes like binoculars, watching me climb toward the moon.

I covered half the distance in no time, and then climbed some more. The lift got even stronger as I soared over the long valley of Pastoria and swerved right to skirt the Temple and came into the amphitheatre over the ridge behind it.

The view was fantastic. A thousand feet below, I saw the flickering lights of the Temple, and above it the blackness of the amphitheatre horseshoed by giant rocks and a protective ridge. A wide, white graveled path led from the Temple to the outdoor theatre, and several smaller paths led down the slope to the village. Up those paths the next morning would come Drago's flock and LaFarge's Untouchables.

I straightened my body and swooped lower toward the slope. Just as I felt the current of air diminish, I twisted, turned, and dove straight down into the void of blackness. The rows of stone pews carved right out of the side of the mountain sailed under me as I sailed toward the platform and the altar above it. The slab of stone was like a stage, with the ridge—also solid stone—as its back wall. The stage was about thirty feet wide and twenty-five feet deep.

If I misjudged my drop I would sail head first into the stone wall.

I didn't. Midway across the platform I pulled up, felt the wind give up on the glider above me, and dropped straight down.

Quickly I collapsed the glider and lay flat on the stone, listening. It was as silent as a tomb, just as I thought it would be. If there were any guards, they would be stationed at the bottom of the cliff behind the amphitheatre. I figured that somewhere in the face of that cliff was the opening into the cavern, or caverns, under where I was standing.

Looking out I could see the tiers of stone seats leading nearly a quarter of a mile to the top of the improvised bowl. Huge speakers were mounted on each side of the stage, and long lines of cable ran back and forth along the rear of it.

To my right, a jumble of rocks projected from the stage for about thirty feet before dropping off the rim of the bowl, which, in turn, ran in a wide arc around all the seats to the other side of the stage. I unhooked the two packs from the glider and headed for the rocks. I scrambled over the smaller ones and peered down.

Perfect.

Between the face of the cliff and the larger rocks was a shelf I could use as a walkway and a place to hide until the moment of my appearance.

I climbed on up the rocks and found more luck running my way. There was a natural bowl in the center of them where I could "appear" in a puff of smoke. I unpacked and started in.

I ringed all the rocks with a mixture of sulphur and flash powder, and then placed the smoke cannisters in appropriate spots so the "hole" from which I would appear would be highly clouded, and also eerily lit with the burning sulphur.

I then led a trail for a fuse down the rocks to the shelf. I also led out the pulls I'd attached to the tabs on the cannisters.

Satisfied that I would either appear as an apparition on the morrow or asphixiate myself with the sulphur smoke and flash powder, I crawled back down from the rocks and to the stage.

From the other pack I took two small kegs of gunpowder and about a hundred feet of wire fuse. I attached the fuse to a remote-battery pack and tossed it back up, over the rocks, to dangle down in my hiding place. I then worked the wire down through the rocks until it was hidden from both the stage and the seats.

Now came the hard part. Using Hugo, I dug a narrow, shallow trench from the rocks to the front of the stage, then a hole in which to bury the two minikegs of gunpowder. Carefully I fused them, and then covered my handiwork.

Just as carefully, I buried the wire in my makeshift trench, and then rewalked the whole area to blot out any signs of tampering.

Finished, I stood on the stage and checked my watch. The whole process had taken exactly one hour.

I was right on time.

I threw the empty pack over the rocks and heard it thud on the shelf. The other, containing the two sulphur and flash powder bombs I'd already rigged in the car, I took with me back to the glider.

I attached the pack back onto the rail and hoisted the whole thing to my shoulders for the climb up the rocky ridge behind the amphitheatre.

It took a half hour, ten minutes longer than I'd expected to gain the top. But once there I felt a sense of relief. The study I'd done on the maps proved correct. The Temple lay about a half mile away and approximately five-hundred feet below me.

I again opened the glider, checked the fittings, and pushed off. I caught the currents immediately and sailed straight out and down.

Guards walked all of the paths between the amphitheatre and the Temple. The moon was bright and I must have been outlined against it like a giant bat. My only hope was that none of them would look up.

In the clearing at the base of the cliff, I saw three big trucks parked, with double the amount of sentries in the rest of the compound. I figured that my original guess was right. Somewhere in that solid rock face was a door, a door big enough for a tank, a plane, and lord knows what else to pass through.

The second landing, on the Temple's roof, was even easier. I had more current to hold me up as I glided in. Again I checked my watch. I'd picked up three minutes. That put me seven past due.

I left the glider intact, anchored it to one of the turret's guard rails, and took the remaining contents of the pack to the edge of the roof.

I had to admit, this whole idea was a little bit crazy, and if Hawk or the sweet Ginger could see me now—walking around the roof of a castle in Southern France costumed in a long black and red opera cape, white tie, and frock coat—they would think me as loony as I hoped Drago actually was.

I crossed from turret to turret until I was sure I was above the right wing and, I hoped, close to the séance room. A window popped easily and I slid through it and dropped into a cell-like room. Two doors and several steps later I was in an eerily lit hall and trying to get my bearings.

I was above the great hall, on the mezzanine level I'd seen the previous evening when Paulina and I had watched the antics of the boy and doped girls. If my calculations were right the room I wanted was on the corner at the far end.

I moved along, staying close to the wall, as far from the railing as possible. The only light was from a few poorly spaced candles, burning dimly but casting protective shadows.

I stopped at the large, oaken door, with a dry, gritty taste in my mouth, and rechecked the hall behind. The statues, in their recessed alcoves, seemed to be grinning at me. I grinned back and slipped into the room.

It was an enormous, low-ceilinged room where the air was close, unmoving, and smelled of incense. Once again, the only illumination was by flickering candlelight. In the center of the room was a long table ringed by several leather chairs. More statues ringed the side walls, and the far wall was an altar affair similar to the one I'd already seen in the great hall.

If this room agreed with most of the others, the

panel would be waist high just to the left of the altar. I grabbed one of the candles and moved to the wall. I played the candle quickly along the panels and frames until I saw it flicker. I found the catch, twisted it, and stepped back as the panel slid open.

Quickly, I rigged the two flash powder and sulphur "bombs" on each side of the panel and trailed the fuse wire through the opening. I moved through it myself and drew a deep breath, then closed the panel behind me.

I sat back, lit a cigarette, and waited for the entrance of Nickrobus . . . alias, me.

Drago was impressive, there was no doubt about that. As I stared at him through the eye of the one-way mirror, I envisioned the charisma the man must have had in years past to establish his first cult, and then do it all over again, here, in Pastoria.

A lot of that charisma was still there, but diminished by age and his state of mind. Also, from the strange look in his eyes as he stared across the table at Serena, I guessed that he was sampling a little of the happy powder he spread around to his subjects.

For ten minutes, since they had entered the room, they had been squabbling like two children. She, contending that the stars and the moon weren't right to converse with the other world. He, insisting that it must be done.

"Don't you see? It *must* be tonight!" he ranted, waving his jewel-bedecked fingers at her and shaking the thick mane of his snow-white hair for emphasis. "The challenge must take place tonight! I must see Lucifer's agent . . . we must confront each other in the morning!" Then he paused, his whole body shaking with tension. "It may be my last chance."

"But, Count Drago. . . ."

"No! It must be now, while my power is strong. We mustn't keep Lucifer waiting, my dear. Wait until you see what I can do. With one simple command—*one,* mind you—I'll dismiss him back to the darkness and his evil master. Like a bothersome insect I will banish him. My power has at last shown me the way. It will be my crowning glory! Now, let's get on with it!"

I agreed. Let's get on with it. Serena obviously didn't want to get on with anything. She was as nervous as a cat on her ninth life.

The old man went on until his voice became a shrill scream. At last she relented and went around the room, snuffing the appropriate candles and setting the stage. Back at the table, she sat and went into her act.

It was the first time I'd seen it, and Serena was a lot better at it than her double had been in London. She started with a few simple incantations, and then her voice seemed to leave her body to float in the air above the table. She tensed and the skin on her bare arms and shoulders rippled as her head whirled around and around. Her hair was knotted in such a way that she could spin it like a black dervish around her head in complete circles.

She was almost convincing me, and she *was* convincing the old man. Drago followed her every move and her every sound. Whatever dope he had dropped earlier only helped. He was practically hypnotized.

·I figured now was the time.

I crossed the wires on the battery pack and all hell broke loose in the room on the other side of the panel. By the time I got it open and stepped through, smoke and blue and green sulphurous fire was thick and shooting ten feet in the air. The smell was horrible and it was all I could do to breathe.

They both sat, staring at what I knew was the vague, hazy shape of the darkly cloaked figure moving toward them through the smoke.

Drago was smiling and nodding in anticipation.

Serena was gaping in wonder.

I grabbed her by the arm and practically lifted her from the chair. When she cleared it I flung her toward the panel behind me.

"How the hell? . . ." she gasped.

"Get going!" I whispered, and stepped into the clearer air by the table.

"Nickrobus," Drago said, and followed it with what sounded like a sigh of relief.

"Rudy Sturgis . . . I am the messenger of Satan! You have summoned me from the darkness of hell!" All of this in the deepest and most sonorous voice I could muster without breathing too much of the vile sulphur fumes.

"I've been expecting you for a long time." His voice was calm now but his eyes were wild and he rubbed his hands together in a way that approached glee.

"My visit was overdue, Rudy Sturgis. You have challenged the laws of my master Satan, and now I've come to claim you for him!" I laid on my best Transylvanian accent and raised my arms under the cape, a la Lugosi. All that, plus the glow of the candles on the green of the rubber mask, had quite an affect.

He stepped back, holding his hands up, palms out in real fear. "No! No, not here, not now!"

"*Now*, Rudy Sturgis!"

"NO! Tomorrow at the Pastoral Sabbath! I'll match my power against you and your master! I confess that now that the time has come . . . that the confrontation is here, I am at peace. I can defeat you! My power is greater. . . ."

He went on ranting, nearly screaming. He'd bought it, hook, line, and sinker. And now he took off as though he were on a pulpit. I let him. His sermon was eating up one hell of a lot of time.

"My Temple will be a trap for your master! I will enslave Satan himself, and the world will be mine!"

He started through Genesis, and I had to admit he knew his Bible. As he paced and roared, I noticed the pulpils in his eyes dilate even further. His was truly mad, and hyped to the ears with dope, a wild combination.

I checked my watch while I did a little cape swirling. Serena had taken more than enough time. Behind me the smoke was clearing. The first layer in the bombs was about burned out. I would have to pop layer number two soon or my eerie light would be gone and I would be just another funny-dressed dude holding a crazy conversation with a wild man.

Drago was really warmed up now, screaming, and approaching Deuteronomy.

Where was Serena?

Then something else was approaching; pounding, running footsteps in the hall. Drago's raving was bringing the palace guard.

I couldn't wait any longer. I still held the ends of the two thin wires in my right hand. I crossed them and again the room just behind me exploded in light and smoke.

When I stepped back into it, Drago took it as a sign of weakness. The fool started coming after me, coughing, spitting, and still shouting.

"You see, my power is stronger than yours! I will defeat you, Nickrobus . . . you and your master! My Temple will be the Satan trap and I will become divine!"

Swell, pal, you do that. Bye.

I practically fell through the panel, and tugged the two smoking cannisters with me. I turned the catch and heard rather than saw it close.

None too soon. Other voices joined Drago's in the room. I used Hugo to jam the catch and moved to my side of the statue's eye.

It was LaFarge, the big Indian Motube, and three of the black-robed Untouchable monks.

LaFarge was gently shaking the older man. "Calm down, Rudy, what is it?"

"He was here! I tell you, he was here! I saw him, I challenged him! You scoffed, but *I* knew. . . ."

"Dammit, who was here, Rudy . . . tell me!"

"Nickrobus, the messenger of Satan! He was right in this room!"

LaFarge and Motubu exchanged knowing looks and nods. The Indian sprinted to the panel, tried it, and whirled. "He's jammed it, probably from the other side."

La Farge nodded at the other three. They ran for the door and he turned back to Drago.

"What did he look like, Rudy? How was he dressed?"

"Like Satan, Harvey, he looked like Satan and he was dressed like Satan!"

I knew where the other three were headed. I hurried down the narrow corridor, jamming each panel with Hugo as I went. Two turns later I found myself on familiar ground. The arrowlike slashes I'd made before gleamed faintly in my penlight. I followed them.

Before I even reached the room, I saw that Serena had done her job. The flickering light through the warped panel of the film and record room wasn't electrical. It was flame, and by the time I got there smoke was also flowing through in even swirls.

I jammed that panel and quickly evaluated. I couldn't go back the way I'd come. By now those corridors would be swarming with Untouchables. But the corridors beyond the record room were foreign to me. I didn't know where the hell they went.

And where was Serena?

Not much choice.

I took off on a dead run into the unknown.

The farther I went, the damper it got. And then the wooden floor became stone and the slant was down. I got the picture completely when the wooden, man-made walls also gave way to stone.

I was leaving the castle itself behind, and descending into the maze of passageways and caves that ran under it. Since all sound was coming from behind me, I kept my light straight ahead and ran like hell.

At a sharp turn, I ran flat up against a crude wooden ladder spiked right into the stone. About thirty yards on down the passageway I saw another. I flashed the light straight up and saw a trapdoor at the top of the ladder.

"Best of all possible worlds," I sighed, and up I went.

The trap raised easily about a foot, and stopped. There was total darkness and no sound. I pushed my face against the opening and threw the light, once, quickly and out.

The trap was being held by the underside of a bed. Pocketing the flash, I worked my free hand up and, after a lot of grunts and groans, managed to move the bed out of the way.

The room was small and perfectly square, with tiny casement windows on either side of the entrance door. A small washroom was set in one corner, closed off by a narrow louvered door. Moonlight glowed brightly through the windows, illuminating a bare stand, the only other piece of furniture in the room besides the steel-frame cot.

There were no pictures or any other adornment on the walls, giving the place a cold, naked feeling like a prison cell.

Or a monk's cell.

I rushed to one of the windows and peered out. Lights blinked in cottages on each side of me. And up the hill about a hundred yards I saw the fortresslike structure of the Temple.

I had been running down hill. Right into the center of Pastoria proper.

CHAPTER TEN

It was about an hour before dawn's first light. Already the paths along the slope leading to the amphitheatre were alive with white-robed figures carrying flickering candles. They were on their way to Pastoral Sabbath and the Count Drago show.

I'd wasted about a half hour in the cottage trying to figure out how to get back to my hiding place in the rocks. The robed figures gave me the way.

I slipped from the cottage and followed one of the paths until some chanting followers got too close behind me. I slipped into some bushes until five white robes followed by two black robes went by.

Evidently, the followers and the Untouchables didn't travel together and, from the look of the procession, the black robes had the right of way.

That meant a black robe for me.

I kept under the cover of the trees and laboriously worked my way around the slope, skirting the Temple until I was on a small ridge behind the amphitheatre, facing the sheer cliff that ran up to its rear.

There were a lot more black robes running up and down the paths here, and there was no slouching, monkish pretense to their movement. They walked upright, with their shoulders squared and their hoods thrown back from their faces. A few of them had even unzipped the front of their robes, letting the garments flop open as they walked. Under the robes I could see gun belts and holsters.

I moved on down through the trees until I was at the very edge of a graveled apron and could go no more. Several huge arcs made daylight out of the whole area, and I could clearly see the trucks I'd spotted earlier. Beyond the trucks, two cavernous doors were swung open and unrobed Untouchables were busily fork-lifting boxes into the opened beds of the trucks.

The boxes were marked in several languages, but they all said the same thing: CAUTION EXPLOSIVES.

LaFarge either had another war coming up or he was getting a shipment ready for one he'd already started.

Footsteps sounded on the path to my right. I hunkered down and peered through the thick underbrush. Two black-robed men came nearly to the edge of the gravel and paused.

"Hold up, I want to finish my cigarette."

"Damn."

"What?"

"I forgot my medallion. Go ahead and finish your smoke. I'll run back and get it."

"Hurry up, we're on duty in five minutes."

"Shit duty. I'm a soldier, not a dock-worker."

"For what we get paid, I'll load trucks from now 'til hell freezes."

"I'll be right back."

"And find out if they've found that guy yet . . . the one the old man thinks is the devil."

One of them moved off up the path and the other settled onto a stump. Idly he watched his comrade go up the path as he dragged deeply on his cigarette and exhaled a cloud of blue-white smoke.

When I was sure the one was out of sight, I slid Hugo free and flipped him, hilt-out, with the blade resting along my palm. It was about twenty-five feet, and very little moonlight penetrated the trees. But the glow of his cigarette would be like a homing device.

Gently, quietly, I lifted my arm up and back and waited and waited. Then there was a slight movement. The faint light moved up and then glowed brightly.

I aimed just below it and three inches my way. He must have sensed or heard the hissing of air as Hugo sailed, because I caught the movement of his head just before he grunted and fell to the ground with a thud.

I was on him in seconds. Hugo had gone clear through his throat cleanly. I pulled, cleaned, and replaced the stiletto. He was about my size, but it hardly made any difference because of the voluminous size of the robe.

I dragged his body a good distance from the path and then strolled across the gravel toward the trucks. Two more figures appeared from the path on my left. They nodded. I returned it and fell in behind them, hoping they were also part of the oncoming shift.

Ahead, through the mammoth steel doors, I could hear the steady hum of a generator. They obviously supplied their own power for the lights, outside the cave and in.

I let the two gain a little ground on me and kept following them. There was a smaller entrance to the right of the big cavern doors. It was a turnstile affair with a glass guardhouse beside it. Behind the glass two watchful guards watched us approach.

I was dead. If some form of recognition was needed for entrance, they would spot me in a second.

I hung back further and watched the two men. Both of them fumbled at their throats beneath their robes and then passed something in front of a beam emanating from just beneath the glass in front of the guards.

I watched the guard's face change complexion from red to a greenish hue as he waved the first man through. When the second stepped to the beam I centered my eyes on his hands.

Then I knew why the nonsmoker on the path had had to return for his medallion. Besides being used for recognition by each other, the Satan medallion was used as a passport to the cavern and probably other security buildings in LaFarge's setup. His army had probably gotten too big for facial recognition, hence the medallion.

I kept walking slowly, with my hand working under the robe, until I fished out one of the three from my own collection.

I passed it in front of the beam and watched the guard's face shift to green. But instead of waving me through, he leaned forward and pushed a button on a console in front of him.

"You know the orders," his voice barked at me from a speaker beside the turnstile.

"What?"

"Around your neck. Keep the medallion around your neck. They're too easy to misplace otherwise."

"Oh, yeah, yeah. Forgot."

"Go ahead!"

I draped the medallion around my neck and moved into a long, steel-sided, steel-floored and steel-ceilinged passageway. The slant was slight for about fifty yards, but I could feel that I was descending.

Another door opened with the medallion and slid shut when I stepped through.

On the map it had been big. In person it was huge, about the length of two football fields and over a hundred feet high. The whole was lit by more arcs mounted into the roof of the cavern, and what they illuminated was mind-boggling. Phantoms and MIGs stood side by side in a long line. They were wingless and tailless, but ready for instant assembly. Fifteen to twenty fully armed tanks from half as many countries stood in a gleaming row.

Missiles and huge crates that probably housed the radar tracking and guidance systems stood among crates of machine guns, rifles, and ammunition for all.

I was on a catwalk looking down at the Fort

Knox of armament. Enough to start ten wars lay beneath. Chances were, arms aid to several countries that had since fallen in the last ten years was assembled in this cavern by LaFarge.

And the wealth he could glean from the sales of all this would be more than enough to buy him a good-sized country.

I could see why Komand wanted back in.

I'd been moving slowly along the catwalk toward the center of the cavern, taking everything in, when the sound of boots on the steel grating in front of me brought me back to the here and now.

He was in fatigues, and a pair of red epaulets on the shoulder shouted officer. I didn't know the military ethic but hoped I was right when I threw him a half-hearted salute.

He returned it and walked on by. I moved a little faster but came up short and at attention when his sharp tone of command hit me.

"Hey, you . . . *soldier!*"

"Sir?" I spun to face him, slightly tensing the muscle in my right forearm just in case I needed Hugo.

"You on duty?"

"Yes, sir!"

"Where?" Where, hell, I couldn't think where I should be. And then he helped me out. "Well? . . . down on the floor, or in the cell block?"

I almost said floor and then remembered Serena. I needed that camera around her neck and the film that was in it. If they had her, she was probably in a cell block.

"Cell block . . . sir!"

"Then get with it," he said, inclining his head

toward a passageway leading off at a right angle from the main cavern. I should have thanked him. He practically told me where the cell block was. "And hurry it up! We've got to be loaded and out of here before that voodoo mess gets started up-stairs!"

"Yes, sir!" I started off and he stopped me again.

"And soldier!"

"Yes, sir?"

"Get out of that crazy get-up when you're down here. Can't tell who the hell anybody is around here!"

"Right away, sir!"

He was mumbling as he moved away. "Hell of a way to run a damn army."

I moved down the passageway. It was clean, well ventilated, and a tube of sheer steel. A pretty penny to construct, and it would have taken some time. LaFarge had planned well.

The tube ended and branched right and left. To the left a door was open, and beyond it I could see barrackslike cubicles. Laughing, the clinking of glasses, and music reached me. I guessed crew's quarters, and turned right.

Good guess. I ran into a steel door with a tiny barred window. I looked. On the other side was a spotless nine-by-twelve room with two tables and a few chairs. A coffee pot bubbled on one table and two uniformed guards sat at the other, playing cards.

I tried the door. It was locked. I was about to call to one of them, when I saw the round steel eye in place of a lock. I passed the medallion in front of it. There was a click and the door slid open on well-greased hinges.

"Well, I say, it's about bloody time!"

"Sorry, sport," I replied. "Got bottled on duty topside searching for one of the old man's demons."

"Damn," the second one hissed, "we spend more time with that old fool and his crazy religion than we do doin' what we get paid for."

He rose and started to leave while the first one eyed me coldly. "Where's Ralph?"

"Sick," I answered. "Think he got a bug. They pulled me off the floor."

"Lucky you," said the one leaving. "Those damn crates get heavy. I had dock duty last month. See you in the morning."

He left and I made motions to remove the robe, but with my back to the remaining guard, and chanced a question, since this was my first night on cell block duty. "How many we got?"

"Just one. The woman they brought down last night."

The words were barely out of his mouth when there was a whir in front of me and a door popped open in the wall.

"There's her supper." He started to rise.

"I'll take it." I pulled the tray from the dumb-waiter and moved to the door, fumbling with the medallion.

"That don't work in here. You gotta use the buttons." He pointed to a console by the table and pushed one. There was a buzz and the door slid toward me. I nodded and stepped through. It slammed behind me and he shouted through the glass over the barred window. "Third cell on the right."

I moved down to the third door. There was no window in this one. It was solid steel. I turned. His face nodded and another buzz slid the cell door to the side.

I waited until his face disappeared, then stepped into the pitch blackness of the cell. There must have been some light but the daytime brightness of the outside room left me momentarily blinded. I tripped over something at my feet and nearly fell. Whatever it was moved, but in the sudden blackness I couldn't tell what it was until I felt a hand on my leg and heard a muffled sob.

"Serena?"

No words. Just another sob.

I fished out my penlight and found her. "Paulina!"

"Nick," she groaned. "Nick, is that you?"

"Yeah, yeah, it's me." I set the tray on the floor and got her to a sitting position. "What happened?"

Instead of answering right away, she found my hand holding the penlight and trained it on her face. "Tell me. . . ."

"Tell you what?"

"My face. What did they do to my face?"

I had to chuckle. She might have been half nymphomaniac and half spy, but she was all movie star. I checked her over. One eye was swollen shut. The other was badly bruised, and both her cheeks were getting blue. There was nothing that wouldn't repair itself in a few weeks and I told her so.

"You have to expect that in the spy business," I said.

"I won't, not anymore, if I get out of this. The hell with Interpol!"

"Give."

"They were checking all the cars coming from the direction of the mountain. Nick, it was the local police. I told them at once who I was, and instead of letting me go on they took me prisoner!"

I nodded. "It figures. They couldn't be operating up here this big, this long without a certain segment of the local law in on it. That's probably why those big trucks can get up here over weight-limit roads without any trouble. Can you stand?"

"I think so."

She could. She was wobbly, but she was up. "Do you remember how you got in here?"

She nodded. "They took me up somewhere by the amphitheatre. There was a door, and a hall, and then an elevator. It must have been a high elevator. I almost lost my stomach."

"It wasn't high, honey, it was low. You're about six hundred feet underground."

She started to talk some more but I shushed her and thought. I had already figured that there was another way out of the cavern. I opted for stairs, but an elevator was perfect.

"Listen, do you think you could find your way back to that elevator from here?"

"Yes, I . . . I'm sure I can. We came up a flight of steel steps, then turned. . . ."

"Save it. Just lead the way when the time comes." I shoved Wilhelmina into her hands. "Can you use this?"

"I don't think so. I've only handled one in a couple of films and I never had to fire it."

Some spy, some cop, I thought.

I switched off the safety. "This is the butt, this is the muzzle. Make sure the muzzle doesn't get pointed at either one of us when you squeeze this. Got it?"

She nodded, a little weakly, but it was a yes nod. I went on to explain how we were going to get past the guard, and then opened my fly.

"What are you *doing?*"

"Preparing a safety measure," I said, palming Pierre and rezipping.

"Down there?" She managed a weak smile even through the cracked lips.

"Just do exactly as I tell you, fast, when the time comes. Let's go."

After checking for his face at the window, I stepped into the block and waved her after me. She skipped ahead of me and to the side until she was flattened against the wall to the side of the door.

"Ready."

The door buzzed and I stepped three-quarters of the way through, anchoring my foot against it as I planted myself.

"She couldn't eat. She was still out."

He looked up, shrugged, and then seemed to have a second thought. "You should have yelled from down in the block. Out or not, we're not supposed to leave a cell door. . . ."

He never finished. Paulina flashed through the door and stood in the center of the room, shakily waving Wilhelmina in his general direction.

"Stick 'em up!"

Oh, my God, stick 'em up? He'll never go for it, I thought, and I was right. His eyes telegraphed a warning and his hand was already moving toward the holstered .45 at his belt.

I swiveled my head toward Paulina. "Shoot him! Pull the trigger!" Her face was stark white and her lips were quivering more than her hands. She couldn't kill anybody and both the guard and myself realized it at the same time.

I hurled the tray at his face and bounced Pierre off the wall close to his head. At the same time I leaped sideways and hoped Paulina wouldn't decide now to pull the trigger.

She didn't. My body block carried us to the floor and we slid into a far corner.

"Don't breathe!"

"Huh?"

"Take one big breath and stop breathing."

She did and I did the same. I covered her just in case he got off one shot before the lethal little gas bomb did its work. He didn't. I heard him gag a few times and then the clatter as his gun hit the steel floor. That sound was quickly followed by the thud of his lifeless body.

Still holding air in my cheeks, to let her know not to breathe, I found the right button on the console to open the outer door. We stepped into the hall and I reclosed it with the medallion.

"Okay, you can breathe."

There was a whoosh and then a river of words. "You killed him! That was some kind of gas, wasn't it? You *killed* him. Couldn't you have just knocked him out or something? Did you have to kill. . . ."

I slapped her twice, hard, rocking her head from shoulder to shoulder. She shut up but the look in her eyes was a mixture of fear and revulsion.

"He was going to kill us, Paulina. This isn't the

movies and there's no silver bullets in this." I
hefted Wilhelmina and stowed her away. "You
should have killed him."

"I couldn't. I couldn't kill anybody."

"Yeah, I know," I said. "Now let's find that
elevator."

She did remember, every step of the way. No one
paid any attention to us, and by way of explanation
to the two guards topside I grunted something
about Drago wanting to use her as an example of
sin.

"I like that," she whispered, as we moved in with
a crowd toward the amphitheatre proper.

"It's better than 'Stick 'em up,' isn't it?" I
grinned.

Again our eyes met and hers fell. I'd reminded
her of what had just happened and she couldn't
take it.

Too bad, I thought, but good in a way. The very
fact that she hadn't been able to kill the guard even
in self-defense was a mark in her favor.

In my mind I struck her off as the one who had
fingered me for Komand.

It was just dawn now, and the crush of people
became a river of humanity flowing toward the entrances to the amphitheatre and the big show. I
held Paulina tightly against me as we climbed with
the crowd. It became a matter of forward five steps
and to the side one.

At last we were close to the mound of rocks that
marked the entrance to the bowl and also became
the extension of the stage. Just as we were about to
be pushed on into the entrance, I stepped free of

the crowd and pulled her after me.

"This way."

"But that's a sheer cliff!"

"Just almost. Follow me!"

No one in the crowd seemed to notice us as I moved around the lower rocks out of sight. Just in case, I checked over my shoulder for some of the black-robed guards. It was a sea of white. All the guards were too far down the hill, by the elevator entrance, to even see us. And, because of the rocks, we couldn't be seen from inside the bowl or the stage at all.

"Step along here . . . this narrow shelf, and don't look down."

She did. "Oh, my God."

I pulled her hard and got her too far along the shelf to turn back. "Now we go up."

"You mean, climb?"

"Just to the top of that bunch of rocks, then over. There's a natural shelf on the other side, between the rocks and the cliff. That's where we'll wait."

She took a deep breath, gritted her teeth, and went up with me right behind her.

In fact, I had the top of my head right against her delightful butt just in case she decided to back out.

CHAPTER ELEVEN

The sound of two thousand chanting, singing voices filled the early morning air and reverberated through the rocks around our hiding place.

"It's like some unholy medieval gathering." She shivered beside me and moved closer. "Like a conclave of sorcerers and witches about to curse us."

"With any luck," I chuckled, "we're going to do the bewitching." I sounded very sure of myself, but, in my mind, I could see that mob gathered in their robes in the bowl below us and could imagine the look on their faces as they gazed up at their leader, ready to do his slightest bidding.

We had already heard Drago's opening speech, or exorcism, and I'd been impressed with the enormity of his power over these people. A cold, unreal feeling settled in the pit of my stomach when I realized that two thousand people would climb these rocks and tear me limb from body if Drago told them that was his divine wish.

I only hoped that both Drago and all his followers had taken their morning soma pill, or whatever dope it was that kept them on the edge of sleeping wakefulness.

Then it was LaFarge's turn. He exhorted the masses to follow the will of Drago and look to the Untouchables as guardians of their divine Pastoria. On and on he went, and I knew that Drago hadn't done it all himself. LaFarge was good. Not as fiery an orator but I could hear the well-disciplined voice of the trained actor coming through.

I shut him off and got my own act together. The costume needed a lot of dusting off and the mask a little repair. From the pack I'd planted earlier I took two elaborate versions of the old fire-shooting Roman candles.

"What are those?" Paulina asked, still a little dazed from her beating and the magnitude of what I was about to do—or try—depending on how you looked at it.

"A magician's manner for the masses," I intoned. "I hope."

I ran dual wires from the two I'd already laid to the bomb in front of the stage, up under my pants and out my sleeves. Then I attached them to the caps of the candles and slid them, in turn, back up my sleeves. I adjusted them so they protruded just beyond the middle fingers of each hand, and hoped the ends wouldn't burn away too far when they started going off.

Satisfied, I turned to Paulina and explained the detonator and when I wanted her to set it off.

"You got it? Timing is important."

She nodded.

Drago had replaced LaFarge at the microphone

and was starting into his spiel about the challenge to Lucifer. When he got going good, I gave Paulina a quick kiss and started up the rocks. It was rough going because the candles in my sleeves kept my arms stiff. By the time I dropped into the hollow from which I would appear, Drago was well on the way to summoning me in the form of Lucifer's messenger, Nickrobus.

I lifted my head over the top, and gasped at the sea of swaying faces and white-robed bodies. On the stage, Drago's aides were pouring white powder into the form of a pentagram. I wasn't sure it was flash powder until I saw a torch being lighted by a black-robed figure behind LaFarge.

And then I saw her. Serena. She was standing beside LaFarge, dressed in one of the white Temple robes. She didn't look afraid, but then she didn't look very at ease, either.

Then a torch was set to the powder and the pentagram came alive. Drago stepped into the center of the geometrical figure and his voice rose to its full oratorical power as he dared Satan to defy his divine power.

The chant was picked up by the swaying bodies in the amphitheatre and, in no time, the noise was deafening.

"I conjure thee, Nickrobus!" Drago screamed. "I conjure thee to appear at my divine command!"

It was time.

I touched the wires and the rocks around me erupted in shooting, multicolored flame. Smoke poured in steady billows around me as I stepped up and then inched to the peak of the topmost rock.

Theatrically, I must have made a fantastic picture as the soft breeze wafted the billowing smoke around me and then away to reveal my presence.

The hordes below me stopped their chanting, and where there had been near bedlam there was now eerie silence.

"I am here, Rudy Sturgis, to claim your soul for my master!" From my height, above the stage and the amphitheatre, the acoustics must have been nearly perfect. My voice rolled like a drum across to the stage, and I saw the people start to mill around in fear.

Below me, I saw a few of the black-robed figures start for their guns and then think better of it. If they started firing into this mob they would start a riot that no one could control.

I was getting no response from Drago so I baited him some more.

"Come, Rudy Sturgis! Step forward and show me your power . . . your *false* power . . . and I will show you the mighty power of my master, Satan!"

That brought a nice gasp from the crowd and a rise, at last, from Drago. But not the kind I wanted or expected.

"I did it. My God, I did it!" He whirled on La-Farge. "You see, Harvey, I told you. I've had the power all along! I'm not a phony. I DID IT!"

He was blowing it, not playing the game the way I'd expected, and the crowd was beginning to wonder what the hell was going on.

I looked back and down at Paulina. She was staring up at me, her smile flattering and her face chalk white.

I prayed, nodded, then sighed when I saw her hands start to move on the detonator.

"Here is the power of Lucifer, Rudy Sturgis!"

I barely got the words out of my mouth before my hands started belching sparks and balls of flame. I used my left arm on the stage and my right into the scattering crowd. If that didn't cause pandemonium, the explosion of the two kegs in front of the stage did.

The earth erupted into the air with a deafening roar. Twin sheets of fire shot straight up and smoke was everywhere. Through it I could see a crater and then light.

My God, I thought, I've blown a hole right into the roof of the cavern below.

"Stay here!" I shouted to Paulina, then shrugged out of the cape and frock coat as I scrambled over the rocks to the stage.

To my right, the masses in the bowl were stampeding in every direction. On the stage, everything was chaos as the soldiers threw off their robes, showing their true colors. This further incensed the crowd and, out of the corner of my eye, I saw white robes enveloping the black ones.

So much for LaFarge's army in the amphitheatre itself.

But the stage platform was a different story. Just as I was about to make the ten-foot-or-so leap, I looked down. There were two of them, one with a drawn .45, the other waving a machine pistol into play.

I dropped to one knee and raised Wilhelmina in both hands. I killed the one with the machine pistol first to stop a spray of bullets that couldn't have missed me. The one with the .45 got off a single shot that chipped a rock by my leg before I dropped him.

I jumped, lit softly, and rolled, coming up with

the spray gun. Four more unfrocked guards—the remainder on the stage—were coming for me, with Drago shouting and waving his arms behind them.

"No, no, you fools! I summoned him and I will defeat him! You will see, my power. . . ."

He never got the rest of it out. Brother LaFarge put a bullet through the back of his head.

Why the four coming for me didn't fire, I'll never know. But I wasn't about to wait to find out. I started left to right and back again. The gun chattered like a runaway typewriter in my hand and they went down like cord wood.

I came up to see Serena running like hell toward me, with Motubu and LaFarge right behind her. If I sprayed too many bullets in their direction I was sure to nail her, too. I dropped the machine pistol in favor of Wilhelmina.

Just as I was sighting in on the big Indian, there was a crack, like a thunderbolt, and the earth—or rather the stage—started weaving like an earthquake beneath my feet.

I looked out and saw the first two rows of seats in the bowl slipping into my bomb crater, which was now ten times larger than before. Now the light was streaming up from the cavern and the hole was plenty big enough to see what had happened.

I didn't know it but the platform of the stage had been undermined by the construction of the ceiling of the cavern. I had placed my homemade bombs immediately adjacent to the two key struts which literally held the stage from plummeting into the cave.

Then I saw it, a jagged crack at the front of the

stage. It was about eight inches wide but spreading by the second. The whole platform was ripping right in half, and when the crack reached midway behind the last support, it would hurtle downward into the cavern. Right on top of everything from crates of heavy-caliber ammunition to surface-to-air missiles.

I didn't know if that would set anything off, but there was a fifty-fifty chance that the whole mountain under us would become a volcano very shortly.

LaFarge and his faithful Indian companion had also seen the split, and decided that escape was a sounder plan than getting myself and Serena. They were scrambling over the outcropping of rocks on the other side of the stage and ramming their way down the path toward the Temple through the crazed mob of white robes.

The lady in question had stumbled and sprawled dangerously close to oblivion. The gap between us was about six feet now and tearing like a slice of dry bread.

"Get up, run, JUMP!"

"I can't," she cried, "it's too far!"

"The hell you can't," I yelled. "If you don't, I'll do you a favor. This is an easier way to go!"

I brought Wilhelmina up and trained the gun on the slope above her left breast. She got the message and backed off about twenty feet.

"Get rid of the robe!"

"I can't, I don't have anything on under it!"

"Believe me, nobody will give a damn." The gap was all of eight now and I could see the steelwork and smoke from the popping arcs and shredding electrical wires in the cavern below.

Serena shucked the robe and came on like a gazelle.

She was lying. She had on a bra and a pair of lacy panties. She closed her eyes and took off like a swan.

I leaned out as far as I could without going over myself and got her by one shoulder and her crotch. I flipped her over and stared down at her closed eyes.

"Did I make it?"

"Yeah. Have you got the camera?"

"What if I don't?"

"I'll drop you."

She opened her eyes and pulled the lumpy right cup of her bra aside. It was full of more than her.

I sat her on her feet and started pulling. "C'mon, let's get the hell out of here."

Paulina had scrambled down from the rocks and awaited us by the path leading down to the elevator. It was fairly clear, other than a few trampled believers.

I led the way and crashed right into a black-robed holdout who'd decided to stay at his post. His face was a mask of indecision as he dumbly held an automatic rifle across his chest.

Not waiting for him to make up his mind, I pumped Wilhelmina twice. Luckily the first one got him. There was no second. I had an empty clip. I'd brought two extras, one in my right pocket and one in my left. I reached for the one in my left, changed my mind, and jacked the one from my right pocket into Wilhelmina's butt.

"Here, you may need this." I flipped Wil to

Serena. She had bared a corpse and was now re-robed.

"I'm shy . . . during the daytime." She caught the gun, flipped off both safeties and expertly pumped a ready shell into the chamber.

I nodded in satisfaction, grabbed the guard's rifle and waved them in behind me. We ran headlong down the path toward the cottages of Pastoria. When we reached level ground, hundreds of drugged followers were milling around looking vacantly at each other. They were mere vegetables without a leader.

"Get on, on down the mountain!" I cried, and then repeated it in as many languages as I knew. "The mountain is going to explode!"

At last they understood and started moving on down, like so many cattle. I fired a few rounds from the automatic weapon over their heads and the stampede began.

We followed them until the graveled path forked. I veered left.

"That's the way back to the Temple!" Serena called.

"I know. LaFarge has another master list of those names he took from Gilda. If he gets away, he can probably start this all up again somewhere."

Serena nodded. Paulina looked confused. And they both followed me.

We had almost reached the graveled parking area in front of the Temple, when something like an atomic bomb went off behind us.

I didn't even bother to look. I knew what was happening, and I knew we were far enough away that little more than a shock wave would reach us.

"God, I can't go any further," Paulina gasped. "My lungs are bursting!"

"Just a little farther," I panted, and leaped a drainage ditch adjacent to the graveled apron.

My feet had barely started crunching on the gravel when I heard the high-powered roar of an engine and a late model Rolls lurched around the corner of the building. Motubu was driving and LaFarge was leaning out the passenger side, trying to steady a .45 in my direction.

I dropped and brought the rifle to my shoulder. Before I got off the first shot I heard the bark of Wilhelmina beside my ear and saw blood spread across LaFarge's shoulder. The gun fell from his hand and he pulled himself back into the car to wave frantically at the Indian.

Motubu was just swerving the big Rolls away from us toward the road when I started stitching bullets across the windshield. It disappeared, but I was sure I'd done no more damage than a few cuts to the occupants.

"C'mon, there must be some kind of a garage around there!"

I sprinted around the corner and practically fell down a ramp into a subterranean garage. There were five vehicles, all late model and all big. I chose a Mercedes limo that was heavy enough to be a tank, and climbed in. The girls clamored in behind me as I frantically searched for a key.

"Over there!"

Serena had spotted a board gleaming with keys by the elevator leading up to the Temple's first floor.

I grabbed them and shuffled through the little

pieces of metal as I ran back to the car. Rolls, no.
Cadillac, no. Jaguar, no. Mercedes, yes!

A minute later we were throwing a sheet of gravel from the back tires and hitting a hundred and
twenty kilometers as I got traction on the asphalt
of the mountain road.

They had about a half mile on us but they were
weaving and their speed was erratic. I floored the
big car and passed the automatic rifle over the seat
to Serena. Beside me, Paulina had her feet on the
dashboard and her eyes closed.

"What's wrong with them?" Serena asked.

"I don't know, but I'd guess I sprayed some
glass in Motubu's eyes."

We were coming up fast and a curve to the left
was just ahead. Just before it, I nosed the Mercedes
to the inside and began banging with my right front
fender. Motubu grabbed a quick look and I knew
my guess was correct. His face was hamburger.

We locked going around the curve and bounced
from the rocks on our left to the guard rail on their
right. Then there was the shearing sound of grinding metal as he sandwiched me against the cliff.

It slowed the Mercedes enough to let him roar
away. Through the back glass I saw them change
sides. LaFarge had a bad shoulder but good eyes.
If I let them get off the mountain there was a good
chance they could leave me in the dust.

Ahead I could see the last dip down, a long
straightaway, with two curves leading into it.

"I'm gonna try once more. Go for their tires
when I get close enough."

Serena didn't bother with the window button.
She just drove the glass out in one solid sheet with

the butt of the rifle, and started firing.

We hit the curve and again I nosed to the inside. If I could force him into the guardrail with the bigger and heavier car, he was finished.

But he fooled me.

When my nose ornament was abreast of the driver's side door, LaFarge slammed on his brakes and I went by him and on into the first curve, bouncing from the rocks to the guardrail.

LaFarge floored the Rolls as we approached the second curve and started playing my game. Only this time the curve was in my favor. Serena emptied the rifle. I heard one of his tires go, but it didn't stop him.

"Use my gun!"

I heard Wilhelmina, and another tire went. Then my gun clicked empty. I knew her job was done, but I passed her my last clip and heard the clicks as she rammed it home.

LaFarge was flat against me now and rocking like crazy. I edged over until sparks started to fly. Just as we entered the curve I veered far to the outside. He was watching me. He was watching the nose of the Mercedes and following it.

That was his mistake.

We were both heading directly for the guardrail. At the last second, I cranked the wheel to the right and slid sideways. The Rolls went on by, slammed the guardrail and paused, teetering, halfway over.

The ass end of the Mercedes came up and gave him a nice, solid nudge. The Rolls stopped us from going over, but the impact was enough to send them hurtling out into space.

I was already backing around and heading on

down the mountain when we heard the explosion.

"Oh, my God," Paulina whimpered, "could they have gotten out?"

"No chance," I replied, throttling down and letting the big car make its own way.

Then I heard it. I leaned across Paulina and looked out the window. A helicopter carrying two men was hovering just to our right, and pacing us.

"Komand?"

"Yeah." I raised back to a sitting position and checked Serena in the rear-view mirror. She was waving, signaling to the helicopter out the broken window with one hand while she leveled Wilhelmina at the back of my head with the other.

"There's a large pull-out at the bottom. Ease into it slowly," she hissed.

"You've been working for him all along. I figured it."

"He was the highest bidder," she smiled. "I hope you understand."

"Oh, I do," I said, returning her smile in the mirror.

"Slow down here!"

I did. About a hundred yards down, the helicopter was settling onto the shoulder of the road.

"If you knew, why did you get me out?" Serena asked.

"I'm all heart," I replied. "And, besides, Paulina here isn't a pro. I needed you to get those pictures of the names, files, and records. No, Serena, I knew from the beginning. You're too good a shot to have missed all of Komand's boys that night. So it stood to reason that you were really the one that Komand wanted me to get into Pastoria. Also, the setup when they tried to blow me apart in the Porsche and later nail me on the highway was pretty clear. You're not too subtle about sex, Serena. How were they going to get you out if I didn't do it?"

"Storm the place," she said. "But when you got through, we figured you might as well do the work."

They were out of the bird now, Komand and the pilot. They stood beside it smiling at us as I turned the car off the road toward them and dropped it into low.

"Don't do it, Nick."

"Got to, Serena."

Paulina screamed as Wilhelmina exploded in the car. The back of my head stung like hell from the blank wadding, and tiny shreds of it showered against the inside of the windshield.

They both rolled to the side. I let the pilot go and went for Komand. At the last second he stopped, knowing it was no use, as the nose of the Mercedes ground him against the helicopter.

I was out of the car in a second and yanking open the back door. Serena, out of frustration and fury, fired again. The wadding burned and scorched my shirt. I yanked the gun away from her with one hand and held out the other.

"Gimme."

"It's worth a quarter of a million!" she cried.

"To Komand. He's dead. Gimme!"

"Can't you give me half that, at least?"

I filled my hand with Hugo and slit the front of her robe down the middle.

"All right, all right."

She pulled aside her bra and handed me the broach/camera. "Damn undependable way to make a living, anyway."

"Out!"

She crawled from the car and stood facing me, one bared breast peeking through the gaping robe. "You gonna kill me?"

"Should I?"

"If you do, I'll come back to haunt you."

"Yeah," I nodded, "you probably would. Go on! Take the St. Tropez fork at the bottom. I'm going to Nice. I don't want to run into you."

She turned, pulled the robe around her, and started walking. About twenty yards away, she turned and waved. "Next time?"

"Next time," I said, pocketing the camera and turning to Paulina. "C'mon."

Dumbly she got out of the car and fell into my arms. "She would really have killed you!"

"That's right." I had a report to file with Andre and some film to develop and dispatch. And then I wanted to get lost for awhile. "You know what?"

"What?"

"I know a marvelous old lady on Majorca who has a villa just inland from Palma. She's a bit of a prude. We'd have to have separate bedrooms. But the butler is a nice guy and she goes to bed early."

"Sounds wonderful," she smiled.

"I might get a phone call in the middle of some night."

She shrugged. "Just so you take my private number with you."